JACK HIGGINS

Ja⋯⋯⋯⋯⋯⋯⋯⋯⋯⋯⋯⋯⋯⋯ age of
⋯⋯⋯⋯⋯⋯⋯⋯⋯⋯⋯⋯⋯een, he spent three
yea⋯⋯⋯⋯the Royal Horse Guards, serving on the East German border during the Cold War. His subsequent employment included occupations as diverse as circus roustabout, truck driver, clerk and, after taking an honours degree in sociology and social psychology, teacher and university lecturer.

The Eagle Has Landed turned him into an international bestselling author, and his novels have since sold over 250 million copies and have been translated into sixty languages. In addition to *The Eagle Has Landed*, ten of them have been made into successful films. His recent bestselling novels include *The Killing Ground*, *Rough Justice*, *A Darker Place*, *The Wolf at the Door*, *The Judas Gate* and *A Devil is Waiting*.

In 1995 Jack Higgins was awarded an honorary doctorate by Leeds Metropolitan University. He is a fellow of the Royal Society of Arts and an expert scuba diver and marksman. He lives on Jersey.

D1144271

Also by Jack Higgins

JACK HIGGINS

Comes the Dark Stranger

HARPER

Harper
An Imprint of HarperCollins*Publishers*
77–85 Fulham Palace Road,
Hammersmith, London W6 8JB

www.harpercollins.co.uk

This paperback edition 2013
1

First published in Great Britain by John Long 1962

Copyright © Harry Patterson 1962

Jack Higgins asserts the moral right to
be identified as the author of this work

A catalogue record for this book is
available from the British Library

ISBN: 978-0-00-727423-9

Set in Sabon LT Std by Palimpsest Book Production Limited,
Falkirk, Stirlingshire

Printed and bound in Great Britain by
Clays Ltd, St Ives plc

MIX
Paper from
responsible sources
FSC
www.fsc.org
FSC˘ C007454

And this one for Sarah

1

He was drowning in a dark pool. The hands of the damned were pulling him down, but he kicked and struggled and fought his way to the surface. There was an agonizing pain in his head. He tried to scream, but when he opened his mouth, water rushed in. And then a faint light appeared. It grew brighter and brighter until suddenly, he broke through to the surface and breathed again.

He was lying on his back in a pool of water beside several overflowing dustbins. The water was filthy and greasy and he closed his eyes for a moment. When he opened them again he saw that he was in a narrow alley with walls of slimy brick on either side, faintly illuminated by the diffused light of a street lamp that stood in the main road a few feet away.

It was raining heavily and the rain felt cool and clean on his face and yet the drops stung him and he couldn't think why. He couldn't remember who he was or how he came to be lying on his back in an alley or why his face hurt when the raindrops splashed against it.

When he tried to sit up he found that his wrists were handcuffed together and there were no shoes on his feet. For some curious reason this didn't bother him. He wasn't alarmed – just slightly puzzled. He frowned and tried to concentrate. It was no good – his mind remained a blank and he became aware of a steady, throbbing pain in his head, slightly above his right eye.

He shifted his shoulders and felt the water seeping through his jacket, cold, sharp and bitter as death. He rolled over and tried to get to his feet, but he hadn't the strength and his whole body shrieked its agony through a thousand tortured nerves.

He reached clumsily with both hands for the edge of one of the bins and heaved himself upright. For a moment he stood there swaying and then he was conscious of a terrible pain in his stomach and he leaned against the wall and was violently sick.

As he turned away from the wall, he lurched into another dustbin. There was a shriek as from a lost soul in hell and a cat sprang from amongst the refuse and disappeared into the gloom. In its flight, it dislodged the dustbin lid, which hit the cobbles with a clatter, rocking backwards and forwards.

The sound resounded from the walls of the narrow alley, mingling with the echoes of the cat's awful cry – and then he was afraid. He remembered who he was and how he had come to be lying, handcuffed and unconscious in an alley and he remembered the most important fact of all. Someone had been murdered and the way things looked, he was the killer.

Panic flickered inside him and he moved along the alley, away from the main road, hobbling painfully in his stockinged feet. He turned a corner and found himself standing under an ancient gas lamp, bracketed to the wall above his head. On the opposite side of the alley there was a door with a decaying sign above it that said: H. JOHNSON AND SON – PANEL BEATERS.

He moved to the door quickly, but he was wasting his time. It was padlocked with stout chains at top and bottom. A few feet away there was a window, and he quickly pushed his elbow through the glass and fumbled for the catch. A moment later he was standing inside in the warm darkness.

A little light filtered through the window from the gas lamp outside and he moved forward cautiously, eyes probing the gloom. He was in what was obviously the workshop. Sheets of metal were standing against one wall and damaged car doors, wings and fenders littered the floor. He moved towards the bench that stood in the centre of the room and a sudden thrill of excitement moved through him as he saw a large guillotine of the type used to cut metal, bolted firmly to one end of the bench.

He slipped his arms under the knife and positioned the steel links that held the handcuffs together over the cutting edge of the base. He held his wrists as far apart as the handcuffs would allow and arched his body over the handle of the blade. Sweat trickled down his forehead and he took a deep breath and pressed downwards sharply. The knife went through the metal link as easily as wire through butter and he stepped back, his hands free.

There were some metal lockers in one corner of the room and he examined them quickly. Most of them were padlocked, but one opened to his touch. Inside he found a tin mug, some greasy overalls and a pair of steel-capped industrial boots. He sat on the edge of the bench and pulled them on. They were a size too large, but he quickly laced them up and moved back to the window.

It was quiet outside and for a moment he listened to the rain drumming into the ground and the faint, faraway sounds of traffic in the main road, before he swung a leg over the sill and scrambled out into the alley.

He pulled the window down and a voice said harshly from the darkness. 'Hold it right there!'

A young constable moved into the lamplight, rain streaming from his cape, and reached out towards him. He moved slightly, the light falling directly on to him, and the constable stood quite still. His face turned yellow and sickly in the lamplight, and there was sudden fear in his eyes. 'My God, Martin Shane!' he said.

Shane didn't give him a chance. His right foot kicked out viciously, the steel toe-cap of the boot catching the constable under one knee so that he screamed and fell back against the wall. There were tears of agony streaming down his face and he fumbled for his whistle with one hand. Shane slammed a fist against the unprotected jaw and turned and ran along the alley towards the main road.

The clock in a shop window said six-thirty. It was that period on a late-autumn evening when the streets are almost deserted. Just after the workers have gone home, but a little before the people bent on pleasure have come out. As he stood staring stupidly at the luminous hands of the clock, the pain in his head suddenly increased and he turned and lurched blindly across the road.

The pain was a living thing and the pavement stretched before him into infinity. He began to move forward, hugging the wall, lurching unsteadily from side to side like a drunken man. The wind lifted into his face and the raindrops stung like pellets of lead. He paused as he came to a brightly lit window and stared into it. There was a tall mirror in the back of the window and a man looked out at him.

Black hair was plastered across the high forehead. One eye was half-closed and the right side of the face was swollen and disfigured by a huge purple bruise. The mouth was smashed and bleeding and the front of the shirt was covered in blood.

For some reason he smiled, and that terrible face creased into a painful grin. As he turned away, a couple passed and he heard a shocked gasp from the woman, followed by a burst of excited conversation. He crossed the road quickly and plunged down a narrow side-street.

He kept on walking as fast as he could, turning from one street into another, moving farther away from the centre of the town. Gradually the streets began to change their character until he was walking through an old-fashioned residential neighbourhood with decaying Victorian houses rearing into the night on each side. The streets were lined with chestnut trees and the pavements were slippery with their leaves. Once or twice he stumbled and almost fell, and each time he had to rest against a garden wall.

The street lamps stretched into the darkness,

and he progressed painfully from one patch of yellow light to the next. As he paused at the end of one street, the insistent jangle of a bell shattered the quiet and a police car turned a corner and came towards him. He dodged through a garden gate and huddled behind a hedge until it had passed. As the sound of the bell faded into the distance, he moved out of the garden and stood on the corner of the street.

The rain suddenly increased in volume, bouncing from the pavement in silver rods. He pulled up his jacket collar and stared about him in desperation, and then, rearing out of the darkness across the road, he saw the dim bulk of a church.

He staggered across the empty street and pushed at an iron gate. It creaked open and he passed inside. A dim light shone from an immense stained-glass window, casting diamond shadows across the tombstones in the churchyard. When he mounted the steps to the door it opened smoothly and quietly as if welcoming him, and he stepped inside.

It was quiet – very quiet. He stood at the end of the aisle and looked down towards the altar and the lamp. For some reason he walked forward, his gaze fixed on the lamp. It seemed to increase in size and to grow small again, and he closed his eyes and breathed deeply for a moment.

A soft Irish voice said, 'Excuse me, but are you all right?'

Shane turned quickly. There was a small chapel on his left, its walls decorated with a half-completed fresco. Standing looking at him was a tall, grey-haired man in overalls with a paint brush in one hand. The overalls were topped by a clerical collar.

Shane moistened his lips and tried to speak, but somehow the words got stuck in his throat and only a dry croak came out. The dizziness hit him again and he swayed forward and grasped at the pew to steady himself. An arm of surprising strength slipped round his shoulders, and he opened his eyes and tried to smile. 'I don't feel so good at the moment. Just let me shelter from the rain for a little while and then I'll move on.'

The priest gave a stifled exclamation as he looked into his face. 'God have mercy on us!'

Shane tried to pull himself free of the encircling arm. 'I'll be all right in a few minutes. Just let me sit down.'

The priest shook his head. 'You need medical attention. You're badly hurt.'

A flicker of panic moved inside Shane and he grabbed at him with shaking hands. 'Don't get the police! Whatever you do, don't get the police!'

The priest looked searchingly at him and smiled gently, so that a peculiarly crooked scar on his right cheek merged with the smile, somehow lighting up the whole face. And then Shane recognized him.

'You're Father Costello,' he said. 'You were a padre with the 52nd Infantry Division in Korea.'

The priest nodded and guided him firmly along the aisle towards a small door in the far corner of the church. 'Yes, I was in Korea. Did we ever meet?'

Shane shook his head. 'No, but I saw you on several occasions.' As the priest opened the door and ushered him through he went on, 'I remember how you got that scar. You went over the top to help a wounded Chinese and he tried to carve you up.'

Father Costello's face clouded and he sighed. 'That's something I prefer to forget.'

He pushed Shane into a chair. They were in the vestry. His cassock hung behind the door and a gas fire spluttered fitfully in one corner. He sat down at a battered walnut desk, unlocked one of its drawers, and took out a bottle of brandy. He poured a generous measure into a glass and smiled. 'That should help things for the moment.'

Shane choked as liquid fire coursed through his veins, and Father Costello pushed a packet of cigarettes towards him and took a first-aid kit from another drawer.

Shane lit a cigarette gratefully, and the priest pulled his chair closer and examined his face. After a slight pause he said, 'You really do need a doctor to attend to this.'

Shane shook his head. 'Not tonight, Father. I've got more important things on my mind.'

Father Costello sighed, and started to work quickly with swabs of cotton wool dipped in aquaflavine. As he fixed surgical tape in position over some of the worst cuts, he said calmly, 'They made rather a mess of you, didn't they? Whoever did it certainly made a thorough job.'

Shane pulled up his sleeves and showed him the steel bracelet encircling each wrist. 'It was a policeman, Father,' he said. 'And they're the toughest of the lot when they really get down to business.'

He stood up and flexed his muscles gingerly. His body felt sore all over, and his kidneys were badly swollen, but as far as he could tell there were no bones broken. He looked at himself in the mirror that hung above the gas fire and turned with a wry grin. 'I'm not sure that I don't look worse now that you've cleaned me up.'

Father Costello smiled faintly and picked up the bottle. 'Another brandy?'

Shane shook his head and moved towards the door. 'No, thanks, Father. I haven't got much time.'

He stretched out his hand to the door-handle, and Father Costello said calmly, 'Don't you think you ought to tell me about it, Martin Shane?'

For a moment Shane was frozen into position, and then he turned warily. 'You know me?'

Father Costello nodded. 'Your picture was in the paper today, and there was an announcement about your escape on the radio.' He took a cigarette from the packet and lit it carefully. 'You know, it sometimes helps to talk with a stranger. We can often see things in a different light.'

Shane moved forward and said tightly, 'This city is crawling with coppers, and they're all looking for me. You know what I'm supposed to have done?'

Father Costello nodded gravely. 'A particularly revolting murder.'

Shane sagged into the chair and fumbled for another cigarette. 'They say I'm insane and I'm not even sure they're wrong any more. Doesn't that frighten you?'

The priest held out a match in a steady hand and shook his head. 'I can't say it does. Perhaps the only person you really frighten is yourself.'

Shane stared into the kindly grey eyes, trying to understand what he was getting at, and then all the fears, all the uncertainties of the past few days welled up inside him and he knew that more than anything else he wanted to pour them out to this man.

He said slowly, 'Maybe if I told you everything right from the beginning it would help. Perhaps I'll get some glimmering of light or see some reason for what happened.'

Father Costello leaned back in his chair and smiled gently. 'I know something of your story from the newspaper accounts, but I think you'd better start by telling me why you came to Burnham in the first place.'

Shane eased his bruised body into a relatively comfortable position. 'That's easy, Father,' he said calmly. 'I came to Burnham to kill a man.'

2

It was raining heavily on the afternoon Shane arrived in Burnham, and there was a touch of fog in the air. As he emerged from the station a gust of wind kicked rain into his face in an oddly menacing manner, as if warning him to turn back before it was too late. He shrugged the feeling off and started to walk along the wet pavement towards the centre of the town.

He found what he was looking for within a matter of minutes, a sleasy, third-rate hotel in a quiet back, street. When he went in a young girl was sitting behind the reception desk reading a magazine. She looked up, a sudden sparkle in her eyes, and smiled brightly.

'I'd like a room for a week,' Shane said.

'With or without a bath?' she asked, twisting the register round and handing him a pen.

He told her he'd have the bath, and she took

down a key, lifted the flap of the reception desk, and led the way up the stairs.

She was wearing a tight skirt and high-heel shoes, and from the rear she presented a not unpleasing picture. The general effect was spoilt by the fact that she had no breasts worth speaking of and a generous sprinkling of acne in the region of her mouth that no amount of make-up could hide.

The carpet was badly worn on the top corridor, and she caught her heel and stumbled so that he had to reach out to prevent her falling. She leaned heavily against him and smiled. 'This is your room, Mr Shane.' She pushed the key into the lock, then stood to one side and he went in.

It was no better and no worse than he had expected. There was a dressing-table and a wardrobe in Victorian mahogany that the management must have picked up cheaply at a sale, but the bed was clean and the bathroom adequate. The room had that unpleasant, musty odour, peculiar to such places and redolent of old sins, and he went to the window and threw it open.

When he turned, the girl was standing just inside the room regarding him with what was supposed to be a mysterious smile. 'Will that be all?' she said.

He moved across the floor, took the key from her hand, and gently pushed her out of the door. 'I'll let you know if I want anything, kid.'

As he closed the door she smiled eagerly. 'If there's anything – anything at all, Mr Shane, just ring.'

It was very quiet in the room when she had gone, and suddenly the pain was with him again, moving inside his skull like a living thing, taking his breath away and sending him reeling into the bathroom.

He quickly turned on the cold tap and filled a glass with water; and then he took a small glass bottle from his pocket and unscrewed the cap with trembling fingers. He poured two red pills into the palm of his hand, hesitated for a moment, and then shook out two more. He crammed them into his mouth and swallowed the water. For a moment longer he stayed there, eyes closed, leaning heavily on the wash-basin, and then he lurched into the other room and fell across the bed.

It was the worst attack he had ever known. He lay with his face turned into the pillow, sweating with fear, and then, abruptly as it had always done before, the pain left him and he could breathe again.

He pushed himself up slowly and sat on the edge of the bed for a few moments with his head in his hands. After a while he reached for his canvas grip and unzipped it. He took out a half-bottle of whisky, pulled the cork, and took a generous swallow.

The liquor seeped through his body, warming him with new life, and he lit a cigarette and peeled off his sweat-soaked shirt. After he had pulled on a clean one he stood in front of the wardrobe mirror and examined his face anxiously. A strong neck lifted from wide shoulders, but the skin of his face was pale and stretched too tightly over the prominent cheek bones.

The eyes were black and expressionless, deep pools set too far back in their sockets. From the right eyebrow a jagged, red scar bisected the high forehead and disappeared into black hair.

He gently traced the course of the scar with one finger, but there was no further pain and he sighed with relief and quickly finished dressing. He pulled on his trench coat, and then he got the glass from the bathroom and poured himself another shot of the whisky.

As he was drinking it he stood looking down at the canvas grip, a slight frown on his face. As if coming to a decision, he finished the whisky in one quick swallow, fumbled in the bottom of the canvas grip, and took out a Luger automatic pistol. He checked the action, then slipped it into his inside breast-pocket and left the room, locking the door behind him.

He walked quickly through the centre of the town, hat pulled down low over his eyes against the heavy rain, hands thrust deep into his pockets.

It had been a long time, and it took him almost an hour to find the place he was looking for. It was a small bar in a back-street not far from the university, and when he went inside the place was deserted except for an old, white-haired barman, who was polishing a glass and listening to the radio.

Shane stood just inside the door, his eyes passing quickly over the old-fashioned Edwardian booths and the leather-covered stools that stood in front of the marble-topped bar. Nothing had changed. He ordered a beer and sat on the stool at the far end of the bar, staring at himself in the ornate gilt mirror and for a brief moment time stood still and he was back eight years. Back to the Monday after the start of the Korean war, sitting on that same stool and listening to the call for volunteers over the radio.

The door swung open behind him, and he turned in alarm as if expecting some ghost from a dead past, but it was only a small man in a wet raincoat and cloth cap, cursing the weather and ordering a drink from the barman. They started a conversation, and Shane took his beer into the telephone booth at the back of the bar and closed the door.

He lit a cigarette and took a small notebook from his pocket. Inside were several names and addresses. The first was that of a man called Henry Faulkner, and he quickly flipped through the telephone book.

17

After a moment he gave a grunt of satisfaction, and compared the address with that in the notebook. A moment later he dialled the number.

It seemed very quiet there in the phone booth, and the ringing at the other end of the wire was from another world. He drummed softly with his fingers on the wall, and after several moments replaced the receiver and dialled the number again. There was still no reply, and after a third attempt he picked up his beer and went back into the bar.

The barman and the other customer were arguing about the probable result of a local football match on Saturday, and Shane stood quietly at the end of the bar, sipping his beer and thinking. Suddenly, he was filled with a distaste for the place. It never paid to return to anything. He had been a fool to come here. He quickly swallowed the rest of his beer and left.

Outside the rain was falling as heavily as ever, and he walked back towards the centre of the town until he came to a taxi rank. He gave the driver Faulkner's address and climbed in.

For five or ten minutes the cab passed through a grimy, industrial neighbourhood of factories, with terraced houses sandwiched in between, and then they turned into a road that wound its way through trees in a zig-zag, climbing higher and higher with each turn, until the city became invisible in the rain below.

Once on top he found himself in another world. A world of quiet streets and gracious houses. The address was in Fairholme Avenue, and Shane told the driver to stop at the end of the street. When the cab had driven away he walked slowly along the pavement, looking for a house called Four Winds.

The houses were typical homes of the wealthy town dweller, large without being mansions, stone built, and standing in their own grounds. The street turned into a quiet cul-de-sac at the far end, and it was there that he found what he was looking for.

The house seemed somehow dead and neglected, the windows staring blindly down at him, and the garden was unkempt and overgrown. He walked along the gravel drive and mounted broad steps to the front door and tried the bell. He could hear it ringing somewhere in the depths of the house, but no one answered. He tried again, keeping his thumb pressed hard against the button for a full minute, but there was no reply.

He went back down the steps and walked across the lawn. Someone had made an attempt to cut it in front of the stone terrace, and a French window stood ajar, one end of a red velvet curtain billowing out into the rain as a sudden gust of wind lifted it.

He paused at the window, peering uncertainly into the darkness of the room beyond, and said softly, 'Is anyone there?'

There was no reply, and he had started to turn away when a high-pitched, querulous voice called, 'Who is it?'

Shane parted the curtains and stepped inside. The room was in half darkness, and it was several moments before his eyes were adjusted to the change of light. He walked forward cautiously, and the voice sounded again, almost at his elbow. 'Here I am, young man.'

Shane swung round quickly. An old man was sitting in a wing-backed chair beside a small table, on which stood a bottle and a glass. There was a rug over his knees, and an old-fashioned quilted dressing-gown was buttoned high around his scrawny neck. When he spoke, his voice was high and cracked, like an old woman's.

'I don't often get visitors,' he said. 'What can I do for you?'

Shane pulled a chair forward and sat down. 'I'm looking for Mr Henry Faulkner.' he said.

The old man leaned forward slightly. 'I'm Henry Faulkner,' he said. 'What do you want to see me about? I don't know you, do I?'

His right cheek twitched convulsively, and his opaque, expressionless eyes seemed to stare blindly into the ashes of life. Shane moistened his lips. 'My name is Shane,' he said. 'Martin Shane. I knew your son in Korea.'

The old man's hands tightened over the malacca

cane he was holding in front of him, and a tremor seemed to move through his entire body. He leaned forward excitedly, and something glowed in his eyes. 'You knew Simon?' he said. 'But that's wonderful. Wonderful.' He leaned back in his chair, and nodded his head several times. 'He was a fine boy. A fine boy. A little wild perhaps, but he never did anyone any harm.' He sighed heavily. 'He was killed, you know. Killed in action.'

Shane lit a cigarette, frowning. 'Is that what they told you?'

The old man nodded vigorously. 'I've got his medals somewhere. I'll get them for you. He was a hero, you know.'

Before Shane could protest, the old man had thrown back the rug and struggled to his feet. He swayed there uncertainly for a moment or so, and then hobbled to the door, leaning heavily on his cane. 'I'll only be a moment,' he said.

The door closed behind him and Shane took out a handkerchief and wiped his forehead. The room was stifling and smelled as if nothing had been dusted for years. He got to his feet and walked slowly round, examining the furniture, and suddenly the old man's voice cracked sharply from the doorway. 'Simon? Is that you, Simon?'

Cold fingers seemed to touch Shane on the face, and he shivered and walked forward slowly. 'Simon's dead, Mr Faulkner,' he said gently.

There was a moment of fragile stillness between them and then twin points of light glowed in the opaque eyes, and the old man's right cheek twitched. 'You're lying,' he said. 'Simon isn't dead. He can't be.'

Shane swallowed, his throat dry. 'He's been dead for seven years.'

The old man's head moved stiffly from side to side like a puppet's, and he seemed to be choking. He backed away through the open door into the hall outside, and his voice was high-pitched and hysterical. 'Keep away from me,' he croaked. 'Keep away from me.' He half raised the cane as if to strike, and then a figure appeared behind him and a woman's voice said calmly, 'Father, what are you doing out of your chair?'

The old man huddled against her like a small child seeking its mother, and she slipped an arm round his shoulder and turned to Shane with a frown. 'Who are you? What do you want?' she demanded, and there was anger in her voice.

He moved forward out of the darkness of the room into the hall. 'My name is Martin Shane,' he said. 'I was a friend of Simon's.'

She stiffened suddenly, and her arm seemed to tighten about her father's shoulders. 'My brother has been dead a long time, Mr Shane,' she said.

He nodded calmly. 'I know. I was with him when he was killed.'

A peculiar expression appeared in her eyes, and she was about to speak when the old man said brokenly, 'Laura!' and sagged against her.

Shane moved forward quickly. 'Can I help?'

She shook her head. 'No, I can manage. I'm used to this. Please wait for me in the drawing-room. I shan't be long.'

She walked slowly with the old man to a door on the other side of the hall and opened it. Shane caught a brief glimpse of a bed against the far wall before the door closed.

He went back into the darkness of the drawing-room and sat in a chair by the window, smoking a cigarette and frowning over what had happened. It was like a jig-saw puzzle with the pieces fitted together the wrong way. The decaying house, the crazy old man and the woman – none of it made any sense.

At that moment she came into the room. She moved over to the window and pulled the curtains to one side, flooding the room with light. 'My father's eyes are very weak,' she explained. 'Too much light is bad for him.'

She took a cigarette from a crumpled packet and Shane gave her a light. 'I'm sorry about your father,' he said. 'I rang the bell and got no answer, and then I noticed the open window.'

She shook her head impatiently. 'It doesn't matter. He's very easily upset these days. He's had

23

a progressive brain disease for the past eight years. He's really only a frightened child.'

She leaned against the French window, staring out into the rain, and Shane examined her closely. He judged her to be about twenty-eight or nine. She was wearing tartan trews and a Spanish shirt knotted at the waist. Her dark hair hung loosely about her face, and there were dark circles under her eyes. As she took another cigarette from the packet he noticed paint stains on her slender hands, and wondered idly what she had been doing.

She spoke sharply, breaking into his reverie. 'And now I think you'd better tell me why you've come here, Mr Shane.'

He shrugged. 'I was Simon's best friend. We joined up together, we fought together. I simply wanted to talk to your father about him.'

She frowned and there was a touch of impatience in her voice. 'Simon was killed seven years ago, Mr Shane. You've certainly taken your time about calling to offer your condolences.'

He glanced up at her quickly, and his face was completely expressionless. 'I'm sorry about that, but I'm afraid I'd no choice.'

There was a moment of silence and she frowned. 'No choice? What on earth are you talking about?'

He got to his feet and moved past her until he was almost standing under the curtain of rain, and his eyes looked out across the garden into the past. 'I've been in an institution for the past six years, Miss Faulkner. They only released me three days ago.'

Her breath hissed sharply between her teeth, and he continued, without turning round. 'Just after your brother was killed I was wounded myself. Shrapnel in the brain. The Chinese got most of it out, but there was one tiny fragment they couldn't touch. It gradually induced progressive amnesia. By the time I was repatriated, I couldn't remember my name. Couldn't even look after myself properly.' He shrugged. 'They put me into an institution. There was nothing else they could do. Any operation was out of the question.'

He was conscious of her hand on his arm, and when he turned, the dark eyes were warm with sympathy. 'How terrible. But you said they released you a few days ago?'

He nodded briefly. 'That's right. I fell downstairs a month ago and sustained severe concussion. Apparently the shrapnel moved. After nearly seven years of living in a fog, I woke up in hospital one morning feeling as good as new.' He grinned somberly. 'The only trouble was that it was June 1952 as far as I was concerned. They had to fill me in on quite a few things.'

There was sudden understanding in her voice. 'I see it all now. The last thing you remember was Simon being killed in the fighting before you were wounded yourself. That's why you came today. To tell us about it.'

He dropped his cigarette into a puddle of water and watched it fizzle out, a slight frown on his brow. After a while he sighed, and turned and looked directly into her face. 'You're right except for one important fact.'

She frowned in puzzlement. 'I'm afraid I don't understand.'

He leaned back against the window and said calmly, 'I mean that you've got it all wrong, Miss Faulkner. You see, your brother wasn't killed in action.'

3

There was a look of complete astonishment on Laura Faulkner's face. For a moment she stared blankly at him and then she frowned. 'I'd prefer to discuss this in complete privacy. I've put my father to bed, but he's perfectly capable of walking in on us at any moment.'

Shane nodded, and she led the way across the room and out into the hall. They passed along a narrow corridor into the kitchen, and she picked up an old raincoat and threw it carelessly over her shoulders.

'I'm afraid you're going to get wet again,' she said, and opened the back door.

The garden fell in several terraces to a low stone wall and a large, wooden hut raised several feet above the ground on stilts. Laura Faulkner ran along the path, her head lowered against the rain, and Shane followed her. They mounted a flight of steps leading to the platform on which the hut was supported, and she opened the door and led the way in.

The far wall of the hut was one great glass window that looked out over a deep valley, through which the river ran towards the town. The view was magnificent. As Shane walked forward there was a menacing growl, and a superb black Dobermann, sprawled across a divan by the window, raised its head and regarded him suspiciously. Laura Faulkner spoke softly to the animal, and threw her raincoat on to a chair.

There were paintings piled untidily in every corner of the room, and a half-finished landscape in oils stood on an easel by the window. Shane lit a cigarette and nodded at the paintings. 'Do you make a living doing this?'

She laughed lightly. 'No, this is a hobby more than anything. I'm a free-lance industrial designer. Anything from furniture to materials.' She pushed the dog to one side and sat down on the divan. 'But we haven't come here to discuss how I make a living. You were saying something rather startling about my brother.'

He nodded. 'What exactly were you told by the War Office when you received news of his death?'

She shrugged. 'That he'd been killed in action in June 1952. On the Yalu River, I think it was.'

Shane took out his notebook and opened it.

Comes the Dark Stranger

'Do these four names mean anything to you?' he said. 'Adam Crowther, Joe Wilby, Reggie Steele or Charles Graham?'

She shook her head, a slight frown on her forehead. 'No, I don't think so. Should they?'

He put the notebook back into his pocket and shrugged. 'They were all with your brother when he died, and they all happen to live in Burnham.'

She frowned again. 'But isn't that rather a coincidence?'

He shook his head. 'When the Korean war started, the Government asked for volunteers. The day that happened, I was sitting in a small bar in a back-street near the university. That's where I first met your brother. I'd just been sacked from my job as a copy-writer with a Manchester advertising firm, and I was passing through Burnham on my way to London. Simon and I started buying each other drinks, and by the time that announcement came over the radio we were both half-drunk. He was fed up with his job, and I didn't have one, so we went down to the recruiting office together.'

'And they accepted you in that state?' she said incredulously.

'Not only us but a dozen more,' he told her, 'and all from Burnham. We were drafted into the same infantry regiment.'

'And you and my brother stuck together all the way through?'

He smiled slightly and unbuttoned his shirt-cuff. When he pulled back his sleeve she saw a green-and-red snake tattooed on his forearm together with the legend: 'Simon and Martin – friends for life.'

Something suspiciously like laughter appeared in her eyes, and her lips quivered. 'Wasn't that rather juvenile?'

He grinned. 'To tell you the truth we were drunk that time as well. We had shore leave in Singapore. It was the last stop before Korea, so . . .' He shrugged. 'We had to be carried back to the ship. When we came to next morning we had a snake each.'

'And what happened after that?' she said.

He shrugged, and lit another cigarette. 'Nothing important. Just the usual things that happen in a war. The front-line, death and violence. Of course the climate didn't help. It's inclined to be cold in Korea during the winter.'

She nodded soberly. 'I believe so. But how did my brother actually die?'

He ran his fingers through his hair, conscious of a faint ache behind his forehead, and frowned slightly as if remembering was an effort. 'A big push was scheduled for our sector of the front. Six hours before the attack was to begin I was sent forward with a patrol consisting of Simon and the four men I mentioned earlier. We were to check on the minefields across the river.'

'And what happened?'

He shrugged. 'We were ambushed. One moment we were advancing through the night, the next they were swarming all over us. We didn't fire a shot.'

'And what did they do with you?' she said.

He thrust his hands deep into his pockets and leaned back against the wall. 'There was a small Buddhist temple not far away. It was the headquarters of a Chinese intelligence officer named Colonel Li.' As he spoke the name, his throat went dry and beads of perspiration sprang to his brow.

She leaned forward in alarm. 'Are you all right?'

He nodded. 'I'm fine, just fine.' He moved past her and stood looking out of the window. 'Colonel Li was an insignificant-looking little man with thick glasses and a club foot. Somehow he'd got wind that the attack was coming, and he wanted to know when. So he started to work on us.'

Laura Faulkner's eyes widened. 'What do you mean – started to work on you?'

He shrugged. 'I should have thought you would have been reasonably familiar with the mediaeval trappings that go with interrogation of prisoners in this delightfully civilized age we live in.'

Her eyes were shadowed and she nodded soberly. 'I see. Go on, please, and don't try to spare my feelings. I'd like to know exactly how it was.'

Shane twisted his mouth into a tight grin. 'On

the first floor of the monastery there was one large room which had previously been the Abbot's. Colonel Li used it for interrogations. Leading from it was a narrow corridor which contained five cells. The monks used to use them as a penance. He made us strip mother-naked in his office, and then had us locked into the cells. Charles Graham and I shared. The others had one each.'

She seemed to find difficulty in speaking. After a few moments she managed to say, 'And what happened then?'

He shook his head. 'We needn't go into details. He came for us, one by one, that club foot of his sliding along the stone flags of the corridor. He tried for three hours, and nobody would talk. Finally he brought Charles Graham back to my cell and told me he was going to start again, only this time he was laying it on the line. Each man would be asked once to speak. If he refused, he would immediately be taken outside and shot.'

'He must have been insane,' she cried in horror.

Shane shook his head and said calmly, 'No, he wasn't insane. I don't even think he derived any conscious pleasure from what he was doing. He was no sadist. That's what made it worse. He was so unbelievably cold-blooded about the whole thing.'

He took out another cigarette and rolled it

between his fingers in an abstracted manner, and she said, 'And this was how Simon died?'

He pushed the cigarette into his mouth and lit it. 'That's right. He was the first to go. I heard the shots fired outside, and some time later Colonel Li came into the cell and told me he'd got the information he required. He said he regretted having had to shoot Simon, but war was war. He almost sounded as if he meant it.'

'And who talked?' Laura Faulkner said quietly.

There was a moment of complete silence as she waited for his answer, and rain tapped against the window with ghostly fingers. He turned slowly, his face calm and expressionless. 'That's what I've come to find out,' he said.

Her eyes widened. 'You mean you don't know?'

He shook his head. 'About two hours later the temple was blasted by American fighter-bombers. That's when the curtains came down for me.'

She got to her feet and, walking across to the easel, stood looking at the unfinished landscape. After a while she said in a peculiar voice, 'Tell me something. What happened to your regiment when it attacked?'

Shane leaned down and gently ruffled the dog's ears with his right hand. 'I found that out yesterday when I called at the War Office. The attack was a complete failure. There were over two hundred casualties.'

She picked up a brush and palette and started to work on the canvas. 'Did you tell anyone at the War Office what you've just told me?'

He shook his head. 'It's been too long. They couldn't do anything about it now if they wanted to. I discovered the other four had survived and were all living in Burnham. The clerk in charge of the records office was most obliging. For some reason he'd got hold of the idea I was trying to arrange a reunion.'

She frowned, concentrating on a particular corner of the canvas, the brush steady in her hand, and said tonelessly, 'And are you?'

He walked across the room and stood behind her right shoulder and examined the painting. 'I want to know who spilled his guts to Colonel Li seven years ago,' he said, and his voice trembled slightly. 'I want to know so bad I can taste it. I know it wasn't me, and it couldn't have been Graham because he was in the cell with me the whole time. That leaves Crowther, Wilby, and Reggie Steele.'

She dropped the palette and brush, and turned swiftly, her eyes flashing. 'And what will you do when you find out?' she said. 'What possible good can it do to know after so many years?'

He started to turn away without answering, and she grabbed for his lapels to hold him. One of her hands knocked against the butt of the Luger, and the breath hissed sharply between her teeth. For a moment she gazed up into his face, horror in her eyes, and then she reached inside his jacket and pulled out the pistol. 'You fool,' she said. 'You stupid, damned fool. What good will this do? Will it bring any of those men back? Will it help Simon?'

He took the Luger gently from her hand and replaced it in his inside pocket. As he buttoned his trench-coat he said quietly, 'Let's just say I'm doing this for myself and leave it at that.'

She turned from him, hands clasped in agony. 'What right have you to come and upset all our lives like this?' she said. 'It's ancient history now. Dead and buried long ago. Why can't you leave it there?'

He ignored her outburst and turned towards the door. As he reached for the handle she cried out sharply, 'They'll hang you! You realize that, don't you?'

A peculiar, twisted smile appeared on his face. 'Sorry to disappoint you,' he said, 'but I'm afraid I shan't be available.'

Something in his voice, some quality of deadness, caused her to shiver uncontrollably. 'What do you mean by that remark?' she said.

'I mean that I'll be dead, Miss Faulkner,' he replied calmly, and there was a hard finality in his tone.

As he opened the door she darted across the

room and caught hold of his arm. 'What are you talking about?' she demanded.

He shrugged. 'That fall I had did more than restore my memory. It moved the shrapnel into a more dangerous area of the brain. It means that an attempt to remove it is essential. I've got a date with a brain surgeon at Guy's Hospital one week from today. If I don't keep that appointment I'll be dead within a fortnight and the odds are a hundred to one against success. Quite a choice, isn't it?'

He walked out on to the veranda without waiting for a reply, and descended the steps to the garden. Behind him Laura Faulkner was crying uncontrollably. He glanced back once and saw her standing in the doorway, the Dobermann by her side, gazing after him.

He followed a path round the side of the house, and when he reached the corner he looked back again, but this time the door to the studio was closed and the veranda deserted.

4

It was still raining heavily as he walked away from the house, and when he reached the main road he hesitated on the corner, looking for a bus stop. There was a small general store opposite, and he bought some cigarettes and checked on Charles Graham's address. It was only a quarter of a mile away on the main road into town, and he decided to walk.

He wondered if Graham had changed much. Seven years was a long time, but then Graham hadn't been very old. He couldn't be more than thirty-two or three now. As he walked along the wet pavement he tried to visualize the others. Wilby, a rough lout of a man with a long record of petty crimes, but a good soldier. Crowther had been a student, fresh from university, and Charles Graham had worked for his uncle, learning to be a wool-broker. And what about

Reggie Steele? Shane tried hard, but was unable to remember.

It was something to which he was becoming accustomed by now, an irritating hangover from his illness that made him forget odd, unimportant things, leaving exasperating blanks in his memory.

He found Graham's place with no difficulty. It was a large and pretentious, late-Victorian town house in grey stone standing remotely in a sea of smooth lawns and flower-beds. It had one unusual feature. Most of the second storey was taken up by a large conservatory, with a terrace that looked out over the valley to the town below.

Shane checked the address again, and then shrugged and walked along the drive to the front door. He pressed a button and a peal of chimes sounded melodiously from somewhere inside. After a moment or two he heard steps approaching. The door opened, a pleasant-faced, motherly looking old woman peered out at him. She was wearing a large white apron and there was flour on her hands.

'I'd like to see Mr Graham if he's at home,' Shane said.

A look of complete astonishment passed across her face. 'But Mr Graham never receives visitors, sir. Not since his trouble. I thought everyone knew that.'

Shane concealed his surprise and smiled pleasantly. 'I think he'll see me if you tell him I'm here.

We're very old friends. I've been away for several years, and we haven't seen each other for quite a while.'

She looked uncertain and wiped her hands on the apron. 'I'll tell Mr Graham you're here, sir, if you insist, but I don't think it'll do any good.'

Shane gave her his name, and she crossed the hall and mounted the broad stairway. He turned to the oak-panelled wall and examined some of the paintings hanging there. They were all excellent, mostly originals, and when his eyes fell on the exquisite Chinese vase on the table by the door he pursed his lips in a soundless whistle. Whatever else had troubled Charles Graham during the past seven years one thing was obvious. It wasn't shortage of money.

There was a slight cough behind him, and he turned to find the old woman standing there, an expression of amazement on her face. 'Mr Graham would like you to come up to the conservatory, sir. It's on the second floor. I'll show you the way.'

He followed her up the thickly carpeted stairs. They passed along a broad corridor and mounted another flight of stairs to the second storey. Facing them was an oak door strengthened with bands of wrought iron, and she opened it and motioned him inside.

Rain drummed steadily against the glass roof, and a brooding quiet hung over everything. it was like stepping into a Turkish bath, and clammy heat enveloped Shane with a heavy hand so that sweat sprang to his brow and he peeled off his coat and draped it over a chair by the door.

The place was like a jungle, a mass of green leaves and trailing vines, topped by a profusion of exotic flowers, and a strange, heady perfume touched everything with invisible fingers, making him feel vaguely uneasy. Over everything there hung the hot, moist smell of the jungle, redolent with decay and rottenness, and he frowned and moved forward along a narrow path.

There was a vague, eerie rustling amongst the leaves on his right as if someone moved there quietly. When he reached the far end of the conservatory he found a table and two basketwork chairs facing the door which gave access to the terrace. There was no sign of Graham.

He hesitated, frowning, and then, as he was about to move forward to look out on to the terrace, he was suddenly aware that he was being watched. He turned and said sharply, 'Is that you, Graham?'

There was a moment of silence and then a low sigh, as if a small wind had moved through the leaves. A voice said in a broken, hoarse whisper, 'I'm sorry, Shane. I had to be sure. I couldn't believe it was really you. I thought you were dead.'

At the sound of that voice Shane started violently.

There was something horrible and uncanny about it. Something that struck a small chord of fear in his heart. He forced a smile, and said in a calm voice, 'It's me all right, Graham.'

There was a slight movement as the leaves in front of him were pushed away, and Graham stepped into view. Shane's eyes widened in horror and the flesh seemed to crawl across his body. The man who faced him had snow-white hair and a face like something out of a nightmare. The eyes gazed steadily at him out of a mass of twisted flesh and scar tissue, and the mouth was like an open wound.

Slowly, horribly, that broken face twisted into a tortured smile, and Graham held out a hand. 'Sorry to shock you like this. Perhaps now you'll understand why I don't encourage visitors.'

Shane took the outstretched hand and swallowed hard. 'I'm sorry, Graham,' he said slowly. 'I didn't know about this. How did it happen?'

Graham shrugged, and motioned him into one of the chairs. 'Never mind about me for the moment,' he said. 'What happened to you? The last I saw, your leg was sticking out from under a pile of rubble after they bombed that damned temple.'

He still spoke in that weird, croaking whisper. Shane offered him a cigarette and said, 'I was badly injured. Mainly the brain. It caused a total blackout. I only regained my memory a few days ago.'

Graham gave him a light and leaned back in his chair. 'It can hardly have been pleasant,' he said, 'but it sounds interesting. Tell me about it?'

Shane looked out across the valley to the town, hidden in the mist and rain below, and started to talk. At first he tried not to look at Graham, but he found it impossible to avoid glancing at him occasionally. Each time he did so he found the other man gazing at him unblinkingly.

When he had finished, Graham sighed heavily. 'So I was right first time. You have been dead in a way. This is a sort of rebirth for you. Very interesting. I'm sure the psychiatrists would find you a fruitful subject for study.'

Shane frowned, and glanced at him sharply. 'What do you mean?'

Graham shrugged. 'An experience like yours would be enough to send a more delicately balanced person completely over the edge of sanity. After all, it must be a hell of a shock to wake up one morning and find you're seven years older. It's a large slice of one's life. Can't you remember any of it?'

Shane shook his head and leaned forward. 'No, I can't remember a thing except what the doctors have told me. But I remember those six hours in the temple before the bombs fell. I remember

Colonel Li and the volley outside when they shot Simon.'

There was a moment of stillness, and Graham said softly, 'So you remember that, do you? You remember our old friend Colonel Li?'

Shane shivered violently. 'I can still hear that club foot of his in my dreams,' he said. 'Sliding along the corridor and halting outside the cell door.'

Graham sighed. 'I must admit I find it difficult to forget him, but other things happened afterwards that pushed his memory well down into my subconscious.'

'And what were those other things?' Shane asked. 'When I checked you through records at the War Office they told me you'd never been a prisoner. They had you listed as wounded in action and medically discharged. That's one thing I couldn't understand.'

Graham shrugged. 'It's very simple really. After the bombing I was pretty dazed but otherwise unhurt. The whole place was a shambles. There didn't seem to be any other survivors and, to be brutally honest, I didn't hang around to look for any. I found our uniforms in what was left of Colonel Li's office. There wasn't much left of the colonel, by the way. I pulled on the first battle-dress that came to hand, and got the hell out of there. They were still raking the place with cannon-fire as I went down the hill.'

'And then what?' Shane asked.

Graham shrugged and took a cigarette from a slim gold case. 'I managed to get across the river.' A faint smile touched his twisted mouth. 'I was about two hundred yards from the Allied lines when I stepped on a land-mine.'

'What a lousy break,' Shane said.

Graham shrugged. 'Anyway, they did their best for me. Not a very good best as you can see, but there wasn't a great deal left for them to work on. I couldn't talk for a year, but finally they brought a German surgeon over and he did some new operation on my vocal chords. Now I can speak after a fashion.'

Shane couldn't think of anything to say. He got to his feet and moved across to the window. 'At least you're not short of money, judging by this place.'

Graham nodded. 'My uncle died the week before that last patrol. Remember when I got the letter from his lawyers? I promised you all one hell of a binge in Tokyo next leave to celebrate. When I got out of hospital I sold out to a combine and bought this house. It was the conservatory that appealed to me. I've made quite a hobby out of orchid cultivation. It's a tricky business, you know.'

'Were you surprised when you heard that Wilby, Crowther, and Steele had survived?' Shane asked.

'That's putting it mildly,' Graham told him. 'Crowther was the first to come home. Apparently he was in a different camp from the other two.'

'Have you seen anything of any of them?' Shane said softly.

Graham shrugged. 'There was a bit about Crowther in the local paper when he came home. I dropped him a line, and asked him to come and see me for old time's sake. It wasn't a very pleasant evening for him, and frankly we didn't seem to have much to say. He got married a couple of years ago. The last I heard, he was a lecturer at the university.'

'What about Wilby and Reggie Steele?' Shane said.

'I never bothered to get in touch with them, not after that uncomfortable evening with Crowther. I saw Wilby one Saturday night about a year ago as I was driving through town. He looked drunk, which was completely in character as I remember him. Steele runs some sort of a club in the town. The Garland Club, I think it's called. Strip shows plus luncheon for tired businessmen. It's the latest thing. I believe it's quite a hot-spot during the evening as well.'

Shane didn't reply. He stayed by the window, staring out into the rain, and after a short silence Graham said, 'Are you going to look them up while you're in town?'

Shane nodded slowly. 'Yes, I'm going to look them up.'

'What is this, a sentimental journey?' Graham said.

Shane spoke without turning round. 'I visited Simon Faulkner's father and sister this afternoon.'

There was a short, evocative silence, and suddenly the air was charged with electricity. 'My God!' Charles Graham said. 'So that's what's brought you back.'

Shane turned slowly and nodded. 'That's right,' he said. 'I want to know who spilled his guts to Colonel Li. It wasn't me, and it couldn't have been you. That leaves Wilby, Crowther, or Steele. Take your pick.'

Graham shook his head. 'You must be crazy. How on earth can you possibly find out? Do you expect the guilty man to break down and confess? And anyway – does it really matter now?'

Shane moved slowly towards him, a frown on his face. 'Does it really matter? Jesus Christ!' he exploded. 'Have you forgotten what happened out there? Have you forgotten what we went through and what they did to Simon?'

Graham looked up at him, a strange expression in his eyes. 'I haven't forgotten,' he said, 'but have you?'

Despite the humid heat, Shane was aware of a strange coldness. He frowned, and said slowly,

'I remember everything that happened on that day.'

Graham shook his head. 'Can you be sure of that? You couldn't remember anything for seven years. How can you be so sure of what happened in the temple? How can you be sure it wasn't you who told Colonel Li what he wanted to know? Maybe it's the one thing your mind doesn't want you to recall.'

For a moment Shane felt as though a giant hand was squeezing his chest so that could not breathe. He struggled for air, throat dry, head turning from side to side, as he tried to speak. He staggered across to the other table, and feverishly poured water from the decanter into a glass. For a moment he choked as the water trickled down his throat, and then suddenly he could breathe again.

He turned back to Graham, his face bone white. 'That's impossible. We were in the same cell together. You know it wasn't me, just as I know it couldn't have been you.'

Graham shook his head gently. 'But I was unconscious when they brought me back from that last interrogation. I was unconscious for almost an hour.'

For a moment Shane looked down into the ravaged face, and then he turned and walked back along the path towards the door. Graham moved surprisingly fast, and by the time Shane was pulling on his coat he was at his side.

'I didn't intend to upset you,' he said hoarsely. 'I was simply trying to show you how impossible the whole thing is.'

Shane tightened his belt and opened the door. 'You haven't upset me,' he said. 'Simply suggested another possibility I should have thought of myself.'

He went down the stairs quickly, Graham at his heels, and when they reached the hall Graham opened the front door and moved on to the front porch with him.

They stood there for a moment, and Shane said, 'You've helped me a lot. I'm grateful for that.'

Graham shook his head, and said sadly, 'What good will it do? Who can it possibly help?'

Shane shrugged, and pulled up the collar of his trenchcoat. His face was savage and bitter. 'I don't know. They say nobody can help the dead, but then I'm a walking dead man, so perhaps I'm an exception. All I do know is that this thing is eating into my guts so that I can't think of anything else. I've got to know which one it was.'

'Even if it should turn out to be yourself?' Graham said.

Shane nodded, the skin stretched tightly across his cheek bones. 'Even if it should turn out to be myself.'

'And when you know, what then?' Charles Graham said softly.

For a moment they stood looking into each other's eyes, and then Shane turned without replying and, descending the steps, walked along the drive towards the gates.

5

When he alighted from a bus in front of the university the rain had almost stopped, but fog crouched at the ends of the streets and the outlines of the houses seemed to blur and become indistinct.

He crossed the road to the porter's lodge at the main entrance and inquired for Adam Crowther. A small, red-faced man in a blue uniform with gold facings, directed him to the Archaeology Department in a side street across the road.

The area behind the university had obviously been a high-class residential quarter some forty or fifty years before. Many of the houses had circular carriage drives and stood in spacious gardens. Most of them seemed to be occupied by one university department or another.

Shane found the Archaeology Department with no trouble and mounted the steps to the entrance. It was dark and gloomy inside with walls painted green and beige. There was no carpet in the hall and as he moved forward, the polished floorboards creaked ominously.

He passed a large notice board and came to the office. He noticed another door a little further along the corridor and saw that Crowther's name was neatly painted in white on a small wooden plaque. He knocked softly and went in.

Crowther was sitting at a desk by the long window, his back half turned to the door as he held a piece of flint up to the light. 'Yes, what is it?' he said and there was impatience in his voice. 'I told you I didn't want to be disturbed this afternoon.'

Shane walked forward slowly until he was standing on the opposite side of the desk. 'Hallo, Crowther,' he said. 'It's been a long time.'

Crowther swivelled sharply in his chair and a look of incredulity appeared on his face. 'By all that's wonderful – Martin Shane. But this is impossible. You're dead, man. You died seven years ago.'

Shane shook his head. 'That's what everybody keeps telling me. I'm beginning to wonder if I'm really here.'

Crowther sat gaping at him, the piece of flint still held between finger and thumb. 'What have you got there?' Shane asked.

'An arrowhead one of my students found on a site we're excavating, Neolithic, I think,'

Crowther replied automatically and then he laughed. 'But what am I burbling about? Sit down, man! Sit down and tell me what you've been doing with yourself since the worst years of our lives? The last I saw of you, you were lying on a stretcher with your head split open. They told me you were dying.'

Shane pulled a chair forward and unbuttoned his coat and grinned. 'They told you wrong. It was pretty bad, but I managed to pull through. It took years in hospital though.' He reached for a cigarette. 'What happened to you? I thought you were dead until I checked at the War Office a few days ago.'

Crowther took out a pipe and started to fill it from a leather pouch. 'When they dug me out after the bombing I was pretty well unharmed. Wilby and Steele were both injured and the Chinese took them away in a field ambulance. I never saw them again.'

'And what did they do with you?' Shane asked.

Crowther shrugged. 'Oh, the usual thing. I joined a column of prisoners and they sent us north. It was rather a long walk. With winter coming on, I can assure you it was anything but pleasant.'

Shane looked around the room and smiled faintly, 'You seem to have done all right for yourself since. The porter told me you were Doctor Crowther now. When did that happen?'

Crowther shrugged. 'A couple of years back. I did some research and it happened to come out right, that's all.' He grinned. 'I'm married now, you know. Got a little girl. You must come out to dinner one night and meet my wife.'

'I'd like that,' Shane said. He got to his feet and walked to a glass case containing specimens. As he examined them he said, 'Do you ever see any of the old bunch?'

Crowther shook his head. 'I visited Charles Graham when I first came home. It was such a harrowing experience, I've never cared to repeat it.'

'I know what you mean,' Shane told him. 'I called on him this morning. What about the other two? Do you ever see anything of them?'

'Not socially, if that's what you mean,' Crowther said. 'I met Reggie Steele in town one day and he asked me to have a drink with him, but I was in a hurry.' He laughed. 'To tell you the truth, I wasn't particularly keen.'

'Why not?' Shane asked, suddenly alert.

Crowther shrugged. 'It's the old story. The man one knew in the army seems a different person out of it.'

Shane looked across at him strangely. 'Doesn't what happened out there mean anything to you at all?'

Crowther looked surprised. 'Korea?' he said. 'It's a fading memory, thank God.'

'And what about the temple and Colonel Li?'

Crowther held another match to the bowl of his pipe. 'It gave me some troubled nights at first, but not for long. It's amazing how quickly nature helps us to forget the really unpleasant things.'

Shane shook his head and said with conviction, 'I can never forget. At nights I think of Li and that damned club foot of his and of Simon Faulkner and what they did to him.' He walked back to his chair and when he sat down, his eyes burned straight into Crowther's. 'Most of all I can't forget that somebody told Li what he wanted to know.' He smiled strangely. 'We never did find out who that person was.'

For a moment Crowther stared at him, his face expressionless and then he laughed lightly. 'No, we never did, did we?'

There was a further moment of silence, pregnant with meaning and Shane said, 'I know it wasn't me and it couldn't have been Graham because he was lying unconscious in my cell at the time.'

Crowther laid his pipe carefully on the desk and leaned back in his chair. He said calmly, 'Are you suggesting it was me, Shane? Is that what you've come to find out after all these years?'

Shane's eyes bored into him. 'Was it?' he said.

There was a sudden, vibrant stillness in the room as the two men sat there, poised on the brink of something terrible and then Crowther laughed shortly and leaned down and unlaced his right shoe. He pulled off the sock and raised his foot so that Shane could see it clearly. There were no toes, just a puckered line of scar tissue. Crowther said, 'Take a good look.'

Shane leaned across, his face expressionless. 'How did it happen?'

Crowther started to pull on his sock. 'On the march north in that prison column. I omitted to tell you they made us walk to China. It took us almost five months. It was a hard winter that year. Most of the men died. I was lucky. All I got was frostbitten toes. When gangrene set in, there was only one thing to do. I sliced them off with a jack-knife.'

He finished lacing his shoe and stood up. He was limping slightly as he came round the desk. 'If it was me, it didn't do me much good, did it?' he said.

Shane stood up and held out his hand. 'No, I don't suppose it did – if it *was* you.'

He walked to the door and as he opened it, Crowther said, 'For God's sake, leave it alone, man. It's dead and buried now. What good can it possibly do anybody to know now?'

Shane turned slowly, a peculiar smile on his face. 'You're the third person today who's said that,' he said. 'I'm beginning to wonder why everybody's so worried.'

Crowther's shoulders sagged and something like despair seemed to appear in his eyes. For a moment longer they looked at each other and then Shane gently closed the door on that haggard face and went away.

6

Joe Wilby lived in Gower Street, a row of crumbling terrace houses near the centre of town in a slum area that was due for demolition. Number fifteen looked as if it might fall down at any minute and the front door was boarded up.

Shane followed a side passage that brought him into a backyard littered with empty tins and refuse of every description. There was a light in the back window and he mounted four stone steps and knocked.

Footsteps approached and the door opened a few inches. A woman's voice said, 'Who is it?'

'I'm looking for Joe Wilby,' Shane said. 'I'm an old friend of his.'

There was the rattle of a chain and the door opened. 'You'd better come in,' she said and walked back along the gloomy corridor.

Shane closed the door and followed. He

wrinkled his nose at the stale smell compounded of cooking odours and urine and shivered in distaste. The woman opened a door, clicked on a light and led the way into a room at the far end of the corridor. It was reasonably clean and comfortable with a carpet on the floor and a double bed against the far wall.

She turned to face him, a large, heavily built woman, nearer forty than thirty and running dangerously to seed. She was still handsome in a bold, coarse sort of way and a sudden smile of interest appeared on her face.

'I'm Joe's wife – Bella,' she said. 'He's not in at the moment. Is there anything *I* can do for you?'

There was an unmistakable invitation in her voice and he grinned. 'My name's Shane,' he said. 'Martin Shane. I was in Korea with your husband. I was just passing through town and I thought I'd look him up.'

'Well, that's nice,' she said. 'Joe never says much about his war service.' She sat on the edge of the bed and smiled. 'Give me a cigarette and come and sit down and tell me all about it.'

She patted the bed beside her and Shane obliged. The gaudy house-coat she was wearing, fell open when she crossed her knees revealing black stockings with white flesh bulging over their tops.

'So you and my Joe were in Korea together?' she said when her cigarette was lit. 'That was a long time ago.'

Shane nodded. 'I've been abroad for a good few years. Just got back to England last week.'

She reached over and squeezed his hand. 'That's a good enough excuse for a little drink, isn't it?' She crossed the room to a cupboard, took out a bottle of gin and two glasses and filled them. She came back to the bed, gave Shane one of the glasses and sat down. 'Here's how,' she said and swallowed the gin.

Shane sipped a little of his and grinned. 'Where is Joe this afternoon – working?'

She shook her head. 'He works evenings as a barman at one of the clubs in town. He's where he is every afternoon at this time. Swilling beer in the local boozer.'

Shane tried to sound sympathetic. 'That must get pretty boring for you.'

She swayed towards him, her mouth slightly parted and placed a hand on his thigh. 'You've no idea how boring it can be,' she said softly.

The outside door crashed open and she moved away quickly as steps sounded in the corridor. As she stood up, the door opened and Wilby lurched into the room.

He was an ox of a man with arms that almost hung down to his knees. His face was sullen and bloated with whisky and he stood there swaying, a nasty gleam in his eye as he looked at them.

'So this is what goes on when I'm out of the way.'

Bella moved towards him and said smoothly, 'This is an old friend of yours, Joe. I've been entertaining him till you got back.'

He grabbed hold of her hair, wrenching back her head. 'That's a likely tale,' he said and then Shane got to his feet and turned so that Wilby could see his face.

There was a moment of utter silence as Wilby's jaw dropped and his face turned a sickly green colour. 'Shane!' he said stupidly. 'Martin Shane!'

'Yes, Joe, it's me,' Shane said.

For a moment longer Wilby stared at him and then he flung his wife through the open door and closed it. 'I thought you were dead,' he said slowly.

Shane shook his head gently. 'You must have been thinking of someone else, Joe. Simon Faulkner maybe. Now he *is* dead, isn't he?'

For a moment Wilby glared at him and then he lurched across to the bed, picked up the gin bottle and held it to his lips. He wiped his mouth with his sleeve and said aggressively. 'Yes, Faulkner's dead. They shot him underneath my window. So what?'

Shane smiled gently. 'I mean that Faulkner's dead and you're not,' he said. 'Doesn't that suggest a certain possibility?'

Wilby's eyes widened and he threw the bottle with a crash against the wall. 'What the hell are you getting at?' he roared. 'What have you come here for? You always were a queer bastard.' He turned and reached for the door handle. 'Go on, get to hell out of here.'

Shane moved quickly. His hand fastened on to Wilby's collar and he pulled the big man backwards and sent him crashing across the room.

Wilby came up from the floor with a rush, his great hands reaching out. Shane waited until he was close and then stepped to one side and hit him in the stomach with all his force. Wilby gave a great sigh and, slowly crumpling at the knees, fell across the bed.

Shane leaned against the mantelpiece and waited. It was several minutes before Wilby sat up, groaning and rubbing his belly and when he looked up there was fear and hatred in his eyes. 'What are you doing here?' he demanded. 'What have you come back for?'

Shane hauled him to his feet. His face was grim and there was iron in his voice. 'I'm looking for the rat who spilled his guts to Colonel Li.'

Sudden fear clouded Wilby's eyes and his jaw went slack. He twisted his head desperately from side to side. 'It wasn't me, Shane,' he said eagerly. 'I kept my mouth shut.'

Shane pulled him close, his eyes boring into the

beer-sodden face and Wilby seemed to go completely to pieces. 'You've got to believe me,' he screamed. 'It wasn't me.'

For a moment longer Shane held him and then he sent him staggering across the room so that he fell across the bed. Wilby lay there sobbing and Shane walked to the door. 'I haven't finished with you yet,' he said ominously. 'I've got someone else to see and then maybe I'll be back.'

He closed the door behind him and turned to find Bella Wilby standing in the darkness of the corridor. 'What the hell's been going on in there?' she demanded. 'I thought you said you and Joe were friends?'

He grinned. 'Why ask me? You were listening at the door, weren't you?' She started to move out of his way with an outraged gasp and he caught hold of her arm and pulled her close. 'Tell him I'm at the Embassy Hotel if he's got anything to say to me.' He left her standing there in the darkness and walked along the corridor and let himself out.

It was still raining and the fog was thicker than ever. He walked quickly towards the centre of the town, thinking about the events of the day. The girl, Graham and Adam Crowther – no link between them and yet they all wanted him to give this thing up. And Wilby was frightened. Really frightened. Was it guilt or was he afraid of something else?

He tried hard, but the dull ache was beginning again, just behind his forehead and he started to walk towards his hotel as the pain began to get worse. The fog swirled around him and somehow he was completely alone and fear moved inside him. The world was a spinning, nebulous illusion with nothing real in it and he lurched across the street in a panic.

As he was about to step on to the opposite pavement, Laura Faulkner walked past him, the Dobermann at her heels. The sight of her was so totally unexpected that he drew back in alarm and she disappeared into the fog. For a moment he remained there and then a car swirled past him, dangerously close, bringing him back to reality. He stepped on to the pavement and hurried after her.

He turned the corner at the end of the street in time to see her climb some steps and enter a door. A lighted glass sign said *Hotel* and he stood at the bottom of the steps, hesitating for a moment, before slowly mounting them and following her inside.

There was a tiny entrance hall and a small reception desk behind which an old man in horn-rimmed spectacles sat reading a newspaper. On the other side of the hall was a door leading to the bar and he walked towards it.

The old man coughed gently. 'Sorry, sir, I'm afraid the bar isn't open until six.'

Shane moved over to the desk. 'I was looking for the young lady who just came in,' he said.

There was a puzzled frown on the old man's face. 'Young lady, sir?'

'Yes, the young lady with the dog,' Shane said impatiently. 'I just saw her come in here.'

The old man put down his newspaper and shook his head. 'I'm sorry, sir. There must be some mistake. I've been sitting here for the past half-hour and you're the first person to come through that door.'

Something cold seemed to touch Shane on the back of the neck and he said slowly, 'But I saw her come in here. I was only a few seconds behind her.'

The old man shook his head and said stubbornly. 'I'm sorry sir. You must be mistaken.'

As he started to pick up his newspaper again, Shane reached across the desk and grabbed hold of his coat, pulling him forward. 'You're lying!' he snarled. 'Laura Faulkner just came through that door. You must have seen her.'

There was fear in the old man's eyes and he pulled himself free and backed away. 'You're crazy,' he said. 'If you don't get out of here I'll send for the police.'

Shane took a deep breath to steady himself and said evenly. 'Look, we can soon prove this one way or the other. Have you got a telephone directory?' The old man produced one from a shelf and pushed it across the desk. Shane quickly flipped through the pages until he found the address. 'Can I use this?' he said, pointing to the telephone on the desk.

'I'll have to get the number for you through the switchboard,' the old man told him, still wary.

Shane gave him the number and waited impatiently while the old man pushed a line into one of the plugs on the switchboard and dialled the number. A moment later he turned and said, 'You're through now, sir.'

Shane lifted the receiver to his ear and listened to the ringing at the other end. Sweat trickled down his brow and he brushed it away in an agony of impatience and then there was a click and Laura Faulkner's voice sounded, remote and cool. 'Hallo, who is that?'

There was a moment of terrible silence as he struggled to speak and then he said, 'Martin Shane here.'

He heard a sudden intake of breath and then her voice sounded in his ear, cool and impersonal again. 'What can I do for you, Mr Shane?'

'It was nothing,' he said. 'Nothing important. I thought I saw you in town a moment ago and I was just ringing to check.'

She sounded puzzled. 'But I haven't been out of the house all day.'

When he answered her, the words almost choked him. 'Sorry I bothered you. It was just a silly mistake.' He dropped the receiver into its cradle and stumbling across the hall, lurched down the steps into the fog.

Something was happening to him that he couldn't understand – something that caused the fear to rise inside him like a black tide that threatened to choke him. He was sure he had seen Laura Faulkner and yet at that moment she was four miles away in another part of the city. There had to be an explanation.

He started to walk rapidly through narrow back streets in the direction of his hotel. The pain in his head was becoming worse and as he turned from one street into another, he paused for a moment and leaned against a lamp-post feeling suddenly faint.

He heard a movement in the fog. He raised his head and listened and then the hair lifted on the back of his neck and he turned cold with fear. Slowly someone was coming towards him. Someone who dragged a club foot behind him that slithered horribly over the wet pavements as he advanced.

Shane started forward into the fog. 'Who's there?' he shouted. The footsteps stopped and there was silence. For a moment he stood there, straining his eyes into the fog and then he turned and ran along the pavement as fast as his legs would carry him.

When he reached the corner at the end of the street, he paused and leaned against the wall sobbing for breath and then, quite close by and hidden by the fog, he heard the sound of the club foot again, sliding over the pavement towards him.

Complete panic took possession of him and he ran along the next street as though the hounds of hell were breathing down his neck. As he turned into the narrow side street leading to his hotel, the pain blossomed inside his head and he gave a cry of agony and staggered on.

He was aware of a figure looming out of the fog on his left and an outstretched foot that sent him crashing headlong to the pavement. He rolled, avoiding a kick aimed at his head and scrambled to his feet, a killing rage erupting inside him. This was something tangible, something he could fight.

He caught a glimpse of a hard, cruel face and cold eyes above the flattened nose of a prize-fighter and ducked as a fist grazed his cheek. He lifted his foot into his assailant's stomach, and the man cried out in agony and doubled over.

He fell back against the wall and Shane grabbed hold of the front of his coat and smashed him against the brickwork. 'Who sent you?' he cried savagely.

The man was struggling for breath, eyes rolling horribly. 'It was Wilby,' he croaked. 'Joe Wilby. He promised me a fiver if I worked you over.'

Shane gave him a push that sent him staggering headlong into the fog, and turned towards the hotel. Wilby could wait. There was something more important to attend to at the moment.

The stairs up to his room seemed to go on for ever, and for a moment he thought he wasn't going to make it. As he opened the door, the pain was so bad that he thought his head was going to burst, and he rushed into the bathroom and grabbed for the bottle of pills. He crammed four into his mouth and swallowed some water.

He moved back into the room towards the bed. As he reached it, coloured lights started to explode in his head and a great pool of inky darkness moved in on him and he plunged into it.

7

It was completely dark when he awoke, and for several minutes he lay on the bed, staring into space and wondering where he was. After a while something clicked inside and he remembered.

He swung his legs to the floor and switched on the bedside lamp. When he glanced at his watch he found to his surprise that it was only six-thirty. He had slept for a little over an hour, and yet he felt curiously refreshed and his headache had gone completely.

He was still wearing his damp trench-coat, and he peeled it off and went into the bathroom. As he ran hot water into the basin, he examined his face in the mirror. There was a slight bruise on his right cheek where his attacker had grazed him with a fist. He touched it gently with a finger, wincing slightly at the pain, and he thought about Joe Wilby and was suddenly angry.

He washed his face quickly and changed into a clean shirt. Five minutes later he left his room and went downstairs. Outside the fog was thicker than ever and a steady drizzle was falling. He pulled his collar up around his neck and walked rapidly through the centre of the town.

The Garland Club was in St Michael's Square, a quiet backwater near the town hall. Its gracious Georgian houses seemed to be mainly occupied as offices by solicitors and other professional men. The Garland Club looked slightly out of character with its neon light and striped awning.

The square was almost deserted, and when Shane mounted the steps to the glass door he found it locked. Inside, a man in red uniform trousers and shirt sleeves was busily mopping the tiled floor, and he came to the door and unlocked it, a look of exasperation on his face.

'Sorry, sir. We don't open until eight.'

Shane stuck his foot quickly in the door. 'I'm not a customer,' he said. 'I'm looking for Mr Steele.'

The man frowned. 'You're wasting your time. He never comes in before nine.'

'Where can I find him?' Shane persisted. 'It's rather urgent. Will he be at home?'

The man shook his head. 'He's usually at his other place at this time. Club Eight it's called.'

Shane pulled his foot away, and the man locked the door and went back to his work.

Shane went into a telephone box and looked the club up in the directory. It was about a mile away on the fringe of the town centre, and he decided to walk.

The entrance was in a seedy street with a wholesale clothing warehouse on one side and an alley on the other. He walked along a narrow, carpetless passage until he came to a door. It refused to open and he knocked.

A tiny grill opened and a pair of hard eyes stared out at him. 'Membership card, please,' a voice said roughly.

Shane shook his head. 'I haven't got one. I'm a friend of Mr Steele's.'

The grill shut and the door opened at once. The man was wearing a greasy dinner jacket and soiled white cricket shirt. His black bow-tie was of the press-stud variety. 'If the boss told you to come, then I guess that's all right,' he said. 'Sign the book, please.'

Shane leaned over the battered desk. He hesitated for a moment, and then wrote 'Raymond Hunt' with a flourish. 'Has Mr Steele been in yet?' he asked as he laid down the pen.

'Not yet, sir,' he man said. 'That'll be ten shillings membership fee, please.' Shane gave him a pound note and told him to keep it. The man grinned, exposing green-encrusted stumps. 'I'll bring you your membership card at the bar, sir,' he said, and moved into his tiny office.

Shane went through a door at the far end of the passage and found himself standing at the top of a short flight of steps. The dance floor was below, ringed by tables tightly packed together. A four-piece band on a tiny rostrum was doing its best to blow the roof off. He descended the steps and went across to the bar in the corner.

The room was far from crowded, and there seemed to be more women than men. He sat on a tall stool in a corner of the bar, his back against the wall. The barman was bending over the sink rinsing a glass, and when he straightened up Shane saw to his surprise that it was Joe Wilby.

An expression of astonishment appeared on Wilby's face, but it was quickly replaced by a scowl. He came forward and leaned across the bar. 'Who the hell told you I worked here?' he demanded. 'Was it Bella?'

'I didn't need any help,' Shane told him. 'I just followed my nose.'

Wilby's great hands gripped the edge of the bar convulsively, and Shane went on, 'By the way, I met a friend of yours this afternoon. He asked me to give you a message. Said he'd had a slight accident and wouldn't be able to collect on that fiver after all.'

Wilby's face seemed to turn purple, and murder shone in his eyes. 'All right, you clever sod. You'll get yours soon enough.'

Shane lit a cigarette and blew a cloud of smoke into Wilby's face. 'Now you're really frightening me.' He smiled contemptuously. 'Get me a beer before I forget myself.'

Wilby brought the drink without another word, and went and stood at the far end of the bar and polished glasses, a scowl on his face. After a moment he seemed to come to a sudden decision. He lifted the flap at the end of the bar, pushed his way through the crowd and disappeared through the entrance.

Shane frowned slightly, wondering what the big man was up to, and then he shrugged and turned to examine the other patrons. Most of the women were obvious prostitutes, heavily made-up, and wearing dresses that stayed just within the bounds of decency.

There was a thin sprinkling of the fat and balding type of commercial traveller, on the loose in a strange town and determined to have his own peculiar version of what constituted a good time. On the whole the men were a rough lot, mostly small-time crooks and back-street toughs from the look of them, all sporting the usual extremes in dress.

There was no sign of Reggie Steele, and as Shane raised his glass to swallow the rest of his beer he became aware of a young woman at his side. She was holding an unlit cigarette in one hand, and looked at him tentatively. He grinned and held out a match for her.

Underneath the make-up she was hardly more than a girl, and there was a certain animal attractiveness about her firm young body. At that moment Wilby shouldered his way through the crowd and went back behind the bar, and Shane grinned at the girl. 'Would you like a drink?'

'I've never been known to refuse.' She sat on the stool next to him. Her tight skirt slid a good four inches above her knees, and she made no attempt to pull it down. 'I'll have a gin and orange, if it's all right with you.'

He gave Wilby the order, and when it came she raised her glass. 'My name's Jenny Green. What's yours? I haven't seen you in here before.'

'Raymond Hunt,' he told her. 'I'm just in town on a visit.'

She leaned across, her blouse gaping so that he could see the deep valley between her breasts. 'We'll have to see what we can do to make your stay a pleasant one.'

Before Shane could reply, there was a tap on his shoulder, and he turned to face the man who had admitted him into the club. He smiled hugely, baring his filthy teeth, and held out a pound note. 'I'm sorry, sir,' he said. 'I've just discovered our membership list is full.'

Wilby was moving round the bar, a policeman's baton in one hand, and a sudden hush fell upon the crowd. Shane decided he'd had enough for one night and took the pound from between the man's fingers.

The girl was already melting into the crowd and he shrugged, strolled past the manager and mounted the steps. The manager walked behind him and when they reached the door, he unlocked it and stood to one side. 'Good night, sir. Sorry we can't oblige.'

'It's been fun,' Shane assured him and went out.

He paused on the corner of the alley to light a cigarette. There was a sudden hiss and Jenny appeared from the fog. 'There's an emergency exit,' she explained. 'In case of cops.'

Shane sighed. 'Now don't start getting any ideas,' he told her.

She grinned. 'Don't flatter yourself. Tell me, what were you doing in there?'

'Looking for Reggie Steele,' he said.

She frowned, suddenly distant. 'Are you a friend of his?'

He shook his head. 'No, I don't think you could describe me as that.'

She was immediately friendly again. 'If he isn't

here by this time he won't be coming. You'll probably find him at the Garland Club by now.'

'And how do I get in there?' he said.

She opened her handbag and took out a small white card. 'You'll have to pay a pound for membership, but if you hand the reception clerk this card, he'll sign you in.'

'Thanks a lot,' Shane said. He started to turn away and then hesitated. 'I hope nobody saw you follow me out. I wouldn't like to see you getting into trouble on my account.'

She grinned, teeth flashing in the darkness. 'You don't need to worry about me. I can take care of myself.'

She leaned back against the wall and pulled him against her. He could feel the warmth of her soft young body and he rested his hands lightly on her shoulders. 'Just tell me one thing,' she said. 'Raymond isn't your real name, is it?'

He smiled down at her. 'No – it's Martin. Martin Shane.'

She nodded soberly. 'Yes, it suits you much better.' She pulled down his head and crushed his mouth against hers and then she pushed him away and hurried back into the alley.

He took out a handkerchief and wiped the lipstick from his mouth. 'Good-bye, Jenny,' he called softly.

'So long, Martin,' her voice replied from the

darkness, and then a door banged and he turned away.

The streets seemed to have come alive as he walked briskly through the centre of town and when he turned into St Michael's Square, he found it crowded with parked cars.

The man who had been mopping up the floor earlier, now stood outside the Garland Club in an imposing red and gold uniform. As Shane approached along the pavement, the doorman opened one of the glass doors and saluted smartly as a tall man in a dark overcoat moved out.

The man raised his wrist to glance at his watch and Shane saw his face clearly in the bright shaft of light from the club doorway. It was Adam Crowther.

As Crowther stepped off the pavement, Shane called out to him and Crowther glanced over his shoulder. He seemed to hesitate for a moment and then he limped heavily across the road and got into a small saloon car. Shane ran forward, but had to jump back quickly out of harm's way as another car flashed past. By that time the saloon car was already moving away and as he watched, it turned the corner and disappeared.

For a little while Shane stood there at the pavement's edge, staring into the night, eyes narrowed as he considered the possible explanations for Crowther's presence at the Garland Club.

Jack Higgins

After a few moments he turned and walked towards the entrance. The whole thing was beginning to get very complicated, he decided and as he passed through the glass doors, there was a frown on his face.

8

A white-haired, foreign-looking man moved forward and said smoothly, 'Members only, sir.'

Shane handed him Jenny Green's card and the man examined it, his face expressionless. 'Will you just step over here and sign the book, sir?' he said, and Shane followed him across to a small reception desk.

He signed his own name and the man examined the entry. When he looked up there was a slight smile on his face. 'The membership fee is one pound, Mr Shane.'

Shane handed him a banknote and the man called a girl over from the cloakroom on the other side of the foyer. As she helped Shane off with his coat he said, 'Didn't I see Mr Crowther leaving the club as I came along the street? Mr Adam Crowther?'

The man frowned slightly as if thinking.

'Mr Crowther, sir? No, I don't think we have a member by that name. He went across to his desk and flicked through the membership book. After a moment he turned, a smile of apology on his face. 'You must have been mistaken, sir. There has been no one by that name in the club tonight.'

Shane thanked him and handed him a pound. The man bowed slightly and stood to one side. 'Thank you very much, sir. I hope you enjoy your evening with us.'

There was some undercurrent of meaning in his voice and when Shane had walked a little way along the corridor he paused and glanced back. The man was looking after him and talking busily into the mouthpiece of a telephone receiver.

Shane moved along the red-carpeted corridor, his senses alert for trouble. As he approached the open door at the far end, there was a burst of applause. He passed through the door and came out on to a tiny balcony.

Wide stairs dropped down into a crowded dining-room. Above the tables there was a raised cat-walk and scantily dressed showgirls were engaged in a dance routine.

A small, bird-like Italian was standing at the top of the stairs watching the show. Out of the corner of his eye he saw Shane and turned quickly his face illuminated by a smile. 'Good evening, sir. Can I get you a table?'

Shane waved him away. 'Not just now. I think I'll have a drink at the bar.'

He went down the stairs and made his way through the crowd to the bar and ordered a drink. When it came, he stood with his back to the bar and looked around him. The customers on the whole looked pretty respectable. Most of them were middle-aged business men who were obviously enjoying themselves hugely. Probably their wives didn't even know they were there.

The noise was deafening. Half a dozen girls came out on to the cat-walk and did a can-can. Shane was almost underneath them and got a pretty good view as they flounced by. They were the usual brassy-faced, tarts with too much make-up and dyed hair. Each time they did a high kick they screamed and shouted as if they were enjoying themselves and the audience applauded loudly.

He stayed there for another half-hour, watching the show and keeping an eye open for Reggie Steele. As he ordered his third drink, he noticed the man who had been at the door standing on the stairs, his eyes travelling round the room. As they met Shane's he started violently and descended into the crowd. Shane watched him thread his way between the tables and disappear through a door at the side of the stage.

At that moment there was a drum roll and a

slim figure appeared on the stage. There was a tremendous burst of cheering from the audience and she paraded along the cat-walk and took up position a few feet away from Shane. Their eyes met and an impudent grin appeared on her face. It was Jenny Green.

She winked and Shane concealed his astonishment and waved to her. She was wearing black fishnet stockings and very little else. A wisp of gold material around her loins gave her some sort of covering and her breasts were tipped with two gold flowers. A curtain descended over the stage and she began to speak.

It was the usual sort of act. Famous women down through the ages. Each time she announced a name, the curtain rose, disclosing a nude tableau and various fleshy young women did their best to depict Eve in the Garden of Eden, Helen of Troy and others.

The whole thing lasted for about ten minutes and the audience applauded each scene wildly. As the curtain descended on the last tableau, Jennie swivelled round, arms extended and bowed. She looked directly at Shane and smiled and then she turned and ran along the cat-walk to the stage and disappeared behind the curtain.

Shane finished his drink and pushed his way through the crowd towards the door at the side of the stage. He opened it and mounted a short flight of steps that carried him into the wings. One or two stage hands lounged against the wall, smoking and chatting. They completely ignored him and he moved past them and mounted a flight of iron stairs.

He came into a corridor, lined with doors and as he walked forward, one of them opened to a burst of laughter and Jenny Green walked out. She turned so quickly they collided and when she looked up at him there was surprise on her face. 'I run into you everywhere,' she said.

He grinned. 'You must have moved fast to get here in time for your show.'

She shrugged. 'There were a few of the girls there. We came together in a taxi.' She smiled impishly. 'You wouldn't be looking for me, would you?'

He shook his head. 'Not tonight, Jenny. I'm looking for Reggie Steele.'

She turned and pointed along the corridor. 'It's the end door. The one with his name on it. You can't miss it.' She grinned. 'I'll see you later, handsome,' and went back into her dressing-room.

He mounted a couple of steps and found himself in another level of the corridor. It was thickly carpeted and facing him was a door on which was inscribed Steele's name in gold lettering.

For a moment he hesitated, listening for some sound through the half open transom and then he was conscious of a movement behind him and turned quickly.

A tall, broad shouldered man was standing two or three feet away, watching him. Dark, wavy hair curled thickly over his forehead and a puckered scar bisected the right cheek, giving him an oddly sinister appearance.

'What's the game, Jack?' he said.

Shane looked him up and down and said coldly, 'I'm looking for Mr Steele – Jack.' An ugly expression appeared in the man's eyes and Shane turned quickly, opened the door and went in.

The room was decorated in cream and gold and a fire flickered in a superb Adam fireplace. Steele was sitting behind a desk, papers spread out before him and he looked up with a start.

For several moments he and Shane looked steadily into each other's eyes and then Steele's mouth twisted into a grin. 'Hallo, Shane, I've been expecting you. What kept you?'

The man behind Shane moved into the room. 'I found this mug standing outside the door listening, boss,' he said.

Steele got to his feet and waved one hand. 'That's all right, Frenchy. Mr Shane and I are old friends. Very old friends.' The door closed quietly as Frenchy retreated and they were alone.

Steele went to a cocktail cabinet and lifted a bottle. 'Whisky all right for you?'

Shane nodded and lit a cigarette. 'I couldn't remember what you looked like,' he said, 'But as soon as I came through that door, I remembered you instantly and everything about you. This is just the sort of thing I used to imagine you being mixed up in.'

Steele handed him a drink and sat down behind the desk again. 'I'm not complaining,' he said. 'I've done very well out of this little set-up.'

His dinner jacket was superbly cut and the cigarette case he produced from his inside pocket was platinum. The clipped moustache gave him a handsome, rakish look, but underneath the full lips the chin was weak and effeminate. He blew a spiral of smoke towards the ceiling. 'I hear you've been causing a bit of a stir over at my other place?'

Shane raised his eyebrows. 'Who told you – Wilby?'

Steele grinned. 'Poor old Joe. You've really frightened him, you know. He seems to think you're going to knock him off at any moment.'

'You know why I'm here then?' Shane said.

Steele nodded casually. 'Yes, he did say something about it.'

'And what about Adam Crowther?' Shane said. 'What did he have to say?'

Steele seemed genuinely surprised. 'What's that supposed to mean? I haven't seen Crowther for months.'

'That's damned funny,' Shane said, 'Considering that I saw him leaving the club not more than half an hour ago.'

Steele shook his head. 'You must have been mistaken.'

Shane clenched his fists and tried to control himself. 'You're lying,' he said.

Steele smiled politely. 'Am I, old man?'

There was a moment's silence and Shane said softly, 'Was it you, Reggie?'

Steele raised his glass and looked straight into his eyes. 'And what if I say it was?'

Shane's hand dipped into his jacket pocket and came out holding the Luger. 'If it was, I'm going to kill you here and now,' he said hoarsely.

Steele gazed into the muzzle of the gun for a moment and then suddenly he threw back his head and laughed. 'No, I didn't talk to that Chinese bastard and even if I had done, I certainly wouldn't tell you.' He leaned across the desk and pushed the barrel of the Luger away from him. 'For God's sake put that thing away before they put you back in the madhouse.'

Shane replaced the Luger in his pocket and walked slowly towards the door. When he reached it he turned and his eyes were burning. 'The minute I prove it's you, I swear I'll kill you,' he said.

Steele laughed lightly and shook his head. 'I know you better than you know yourself, Shane.

Killing Chinese in Korea was one thing, but killing me now in cold blood would be quite another. You'll never summon up the nerve to pull that trigger until you're absolutely sure and you'll never be able to get your proof. It's been too long.'

Shane shook his head and said coldly, 'I'll get my proof and if it turns out to be you, I'll be coming for you.' He closed the door and moved along the corridor.

Jenny Green was leaning in the open doorway of her dressing-room and as he approached, she grinned. 'You look like a wet weekend.'

He tried to smile. 'I'm tired, that's all.'

She slipped one of the club cards into his hand. 'I've written my address on the other side. Just in case you feel like calling.'

There was a slight movement behind and Shane turned quickly and found Frenchy standing watching them. 'Is this mug bothering you, kid?' he said to Jenny.

There was fear in her eyes and she shook her head quickly. 'No, Frenchy, it's all right. Just a friend.' She smiled briefly at Shane, and disappeared into her dressing-room, closing the door.

As Shane started to move away, Frenchy grabbed his arm. 'Mr Steele doesn't like people to bother the girls, Jack.' His fingers felt like steel bands as he deliberately exerted all his considerable strength.

'I wish you wouldn't call me Jack. It isn't my

name,' Shane said coolly. His free hand darted forward and fastened around Frenchy's left arm just below the elbow, his thumb biting into the pressure point.

An expression of purest agony flooded over Frenchy's face and as he staggered back, Shane kicked him under the left knee-cap. He left him there, half-collapsed against the wall, mouthing obscenities and went down the steps that led to the stage.

It was only a little after nine when he left the club and walked back through the streets to his hotel. The fog seemed to move in on him with a terrible weightless pressure that made him dizzy and light-headed.

There was a dull ache behind his eyes and he felt weak and drained of all emotion. He got his key from the night porter at the desk and mounted the stairs to his room.

It was quiet in there – too quiet and he was filled with a vague irrational unease. He lay on the bed in the dark and when he closed his eyes, coloured images flashed through his mind and night had a thousand faces.

He had been lying there for five or ten minutes only when he heard a sound that made the flesh crawl across his body. Someone was moving across the floor of the room upstairs. Someone who dragged one foot behind him that slithered horribly over the floor.

He lay there for several moments slightly raised on one arm, staring up at the ceiling, the hair lifting on the back of his neck. As the cold fear surged into his mouth, he scrambled from his bed, wrenched open his door and ran along the corridor looking for the stairs which led to the next floor.

There were no stairs, but at the end of the corridor he found a door which was locked. He pulled at it vainly for a moment or two and then hurried downstairs to the hall and went to the desk.

'I want to know who's staying in the room above mine,' he said.

The porter looked at him in astonishment. 'But there isn't anyone in a room above you, sir. There's only the attics up there.'

'But I can hear someone walking about above my room,' Shane persisted.

The man shook his head. 'That's impossible sir. The door to the top stairs is locked and there's only one key. I've got it here.'

He lifted it down from a nail and held it up. Shane's stomach was suddenly empty and for a moment he closed his eyes. When he opened them again he said carefully, 'Would you mind if we take a look? I'm almost certain I heard someone moving about up there.'

The man nodded and lifted the flap of the counter. 'Certainly, sir. I'll come up with you myself.'

They went up to the top corridor and the porter unlocked the door which gave access to the attic stairs. He switched on a light and went up cautiously, Shane at his heels. When they reached the top, they crossed a small landing and entered an attic which stretched the length of the building. It was completely empty, the harsh light of a naked bulb reaching into the farthest corners.

The porter turned with a little laugh. 'Well, there you are. There's no one up here. You must have imagined it, sir.'

Shane nodded slowly and led the way back downstairs. He waited for the porter to lock the door and then walked along the corridor with him. When they reached the stairhead he said, 'I'm sorry I troubled you.'

The porter looked at him searchingly. 'Excuse me for mentioning it, sir, but you don't look too good to me. Is there anything I can get you?'

Shane shook his head and moved across to the door of his room.

'I'll be all right when I've had some sleep,' he said. 'I'm rather tired – that's all.'

He closed the door of his room and stood with his back to it and waited, but there was no sound and only the quiet shadows waited for him in the corners of the room. He went and sat on the edge of the bed and smoked a cigarette, his head spinning. There had to be a rational explanation because if for one moment he dared to admit to the possibility that he had imagined the whole thing, he was lost.

He drew the smoke deep into his lungs and tried to steady himself. All that was needed was someone with a key to the attic door. Someone who was interested in frightening him away or in driving him insane, perhaps. Whoever it was would have had ample time to leave the attics while he had gone down to the hall for the porter.

He went out into the corridor and moved along to the end. He tried the door to the attics again, but it was securely locked. There was another door behind him and he opened it and discovered a dark flight of stairs which he descended quickly.

A stale smell of cooking rose to greet him and somewhere along a dimly lit passage he heard voices and the clatter of pans. A door faced him and when he opened it he looked out into the alley at the side of the hotel. He closed the door again and went back upstairs, his mind working furiously.

It had to be someone he had met that day, someone who wanted to frighten him because they themselves were afraid. And then he remembered Adam Crowther. He had certainly lied about his association with Steele and if he had nothing to hide, why had he so deliberately avoided a meeting outside the Garland Club?

For a little while longer Shane stood just inside his room, a frown wrinkling his brow as he thought about the whole thing and then he came to a sudden decision and reached for his trench-coat. A moment later he closed the door behind him and went quickly downstairs.

To save time he took a cab from a rank in the centre of the town. Crowther's address was in a quiet residential district not far from the university, and Shane told the driver to stop at the end of the street and walked the rest of the way, his collar pulled up against the rain.

The place he was looking for turned out to be a bungalow, a modern Canadian-style place in mellow brick, pine board, and rough stone. It was sandwiched in between two large town houses in grey stone, each standing remotely in a sea of smooth lawns and flower-beds.

Shane walked slowly up the drive and mounted a flight of shallow steps to the porch. He pressed the door-bell and waited. After a moment the porch was flooded with light. Out of the corner of one eye he became aware of a movement in the window of the lounge. A curtain fluttered, and as he turned his head a figure drew back into the darkness of the room and a hand twitched the curtain back into place.

He waited for the door to open, but nothing happened. After a while he pressed the door-bell again, keeping his finger on the button, and the shrill clangour echoed through the house. A moment later he heard steps approaching and the door opened.

A pleasant, dark-haired young woman with candid grey eyes and a firm mouth looked out at him inquiringly. 'Yes, what is it?'

'Mrs Crowther?' Shane said, and when she nodded went on, 'My name is Shane – Martin Shane. I'm an old friend of your husband's. I wonder if I might speak to him?'

She hesitated, and a slight frown appeared on her face. 'I'm afraid that isn't possible, Mr Shane,' she said. 'Adam came home from the university this evening with a temperature, and went straight to bed. He's sound asleep at the moment.'

'I'm sorry to hear that,' Shane told her. 'Nothing serious, I hope?'

'Oh, no,' she said hastily. 'A touch of flu, I think.' She pushed back a tendril of dark hair with one hand. 'I'm sorry you've had a wasted journey, Mr Shane. Perhaps if you were to phone Adam at his office in two or three days. He might be all right then.' She sounded genuinely sorry.

Shane smiled at her. 'Yes, I think I'll do that, Mrs Crowther. Give Adam my regards, and tell him I'll be getting in touch with him.'

He went down the steps quickly, and walked towards the gate. When he reached it he looked back. She was still standing on the porch, gazing after him, but as he started to walk away she went inside, and a moment later the porch light went out.

Shane stood in the shadow of the garden wall for two or three minutes, and then he went back up to the bungalow, walking on the grass verge. The woman had been lying, he was certain of that. Not only did Adam Crowther not want to speak to him, he wanted it to appear that he hadn't left home all evening, and for that he had to have a reason.

Shane crossed quickly to the flat-roofed brick garage which stood at one side of the bungalow. The door was unlocked, and he opened it quickly and went inside. He struck a match and held it above his head. Crowther's car stood before him, a small dark saloon, and it was still wet from the rain.

As the match extinguished itself Shane turned and went back outside. That settled it. It had been Crowther he had seen leaving the Garland Club.

He went round the side of the house. The kitchen was in darkness, but the rear door opened to his touch and he passed inside. He stood listening intently, and faintly from somewhere at the front of the house he could hear voices. He went forward cautiously, and passed along a narrow corridor which emptied into the hall. Light showed beneath the crack at the bottom of a door on his left-hand side, and he went closer and listened.

Crowther and his wife were arguing about something. She was pleading with him, her voice low and desperate. It was impossible to tell what they were saying, but suddenly Crowther said 'No!' very loudly. There was a sudden unexpected movement, and the door was flung open and Mrs Crowther appeared.

As she saw Shane she raised a hand to her mouth and screamed. Shane pushed her gently back into the room, and moved after her, closing the door behind him.

Adam Crowther was standing by the fire-place filling his pipe from an old leather pouch. He stared at Shane in astonishment, and then anger appeared on his face. He dropped the pipe on to a small coffee-table, and came forward, fists clenched. 'I'll give you about ten seconds to get out of here,' he said.

Shane leaned against the door and regarded him calmly. 'Not until I've had some answers,' he said. 'Such as why your wife just lied to me.'

Crowther paused a few feet away. 'I didn't want to speak to you again. I should have thought that would have been sufficiently obvious.'

'Is that why you wouldn't stop to talk to me when I saw you outside the Garland Club?' Shane said.

Crowther frowned. 'I don't know what you're talking about.'

Shane shook his head. 'You're lying, Crowther, just as you were lying this afternoon when you told me you and Steele weren't friends. You visited him tonight at the Garland Club.'

'You must be out of your head.' Crowther laughed contemptuously. 'I haven't been out of the house all night.'

'You visited Steele at the Garland Club,' Shane said calmly. 'Afterwards you went to my hotel and tried to frighten the life out of me. But you tried that on earlier today, didn't you, Crowther? You followed me all over town dragging that blasted foot of yours, trying to make me think it was someone else.'

There was a moment of stillness as he looked searchingly into the other man's eyes, and then Crowther said quietly. 'What are you afraid of, Shane? Who did you think was following you in the fog?'

Cold sweat sprang in great beads to Shane's face. 'Colonel Li,' he whispered hoarsely.

Crowther shook his head. 'But he died a long time ago, Shane. A very long time ago.' He smiled gently. 'You need a doctor, my friend.'

A sudden cold terror moved inside Shane, and his hands started to tremble. 'It was you,' he said. 'It has to be you.'

98

Mrs Crowther moved forward quickly and laid a hand on his sleeve. There was something close to pity in her eyes as she gazed up at him and shook her head. 'But my husband is telling the truth, Mr Shane,' she said. 'He hasn't been out of this house all night.'

For a moment Shane looked down into those candid grey eyes, a sudden emptiness inside him, and then he remembered. He gripped her arm and pulled her close. 'But I've been into the garage,' he said. 'I've checked the car. It's still wet from the rain. You forgot about that.'

She moaned suddenly, and beat at his chest with her free hand. 'My arm, you're hurting my arm.'

As Crowther started forward with a roar of rage, Shane flung the woman to one side and went to meet him. He ducked under Crowther's arm, and then turned and pushed him solidly in the back so the other man staggered wildly across the room, his hands clawing at an old-fashioned mahogany desk to keep his balance.

As Shane went towards him Crowther moved quickly round to the other side of the desk, and jerked open a drawer. His hand scrabbled wildly amongst a pile of documents, and when it came out he was holding a .38 Webley revolver.

Shane took a deep breath, and stopped dead in his tracks. 'You got a licence for that?' he said softly.

Crowther held the revolver steady, and there was a quiet desperation in his eyes. 'If you know what's good for you, you'll get out of here before this thing goes off.'

Mrs Crowther gave a sudden gasp and came forward quickly. She touched Shane on the arm and said pleadingly. 'Please go now. Please go before he does something we'll all regret.'

For a little while Shane looked down into her frightened face, and then he walked slowly across the room and out into the hall. She opened the door for him and he moved out on to the porch. When he turned, Crowther was standing in the hall, the revolver hanging limply from his right hand. He said deliberately, 'Don't come back, Shane. Don't ever come back. Get out of Burnham.'

For a long moment they looked into each other's eyes, and then Shane turned away and walked down towards the gate, and behind him the woman started to cry.

The sound of that crying seemed to pursue him all the way back to the hotel, and when he reached his room he sat on the edge of the bed, his head spinning, so that he could not make sense of any of it.

He lit a cigarette and lay back against the pillows, staring up into the darkness, and after a while there was a light tap at the door and he ran his fingers through his hair and got to his feet.

When he opened the door, Laura Faulkner was standing there.

He stood to one side, and she walked past him into the room. He closed the door and said, 'How did you find me?'

She shrugged. 'It was easy. I worked my way through the classified directory, telephoning each hotel in turn.'

He frowned. 'You must have wanted to see me pretty badly.'

'I was worried about you,' she said. 'Especially after that phone call this afternoon.'

He laughed lightly. 'It didn't mean a thing. I thought I saw you in town, that's all, and I wanted to make sure.'

She was wearing a loose, open coat over a black cocktail dress that moulded her exquisite figure. Her dark hair hung down to her shoulders, framing the lovely face and she had brought a faint trace of delicate perfume into the room that set his nerves tingling.

'Who's looking after your father?' he said. 'Or is he fit to be left on his own?'

She shook her head. 'I arrange for the cleaning woman to come in if I want to go out. She's very dependable. I was supposed to go to a party at a friend's house tonight, but I changed my mind.'

'Because of me?' Shane said.

'Because of you.'

There was a moment of fragile stillness between them, and she seemed to sway towards him, and then there was a sudden excited whining at the door and a scratching sound.

She laughed lightly. 'Oh, damn that dog. I left him to look after the car.'

She opened the door, and the Dobermann slipped into the room like a black shadow and sniffed suspiciously at Shane's shoes before going to his mistress.

For some inexplicable reason Shane felt alive again. He reached for his jacket, and said, 'It seems I've spoilt your evening. Is there anywhere reasonable you'd like to go for a drink and a dance perhaps?'

She smiled warmly. 'I'd like that. I'd like that a lot.' She appeared to think for a moment and nodded her head. 'I know just the place. It's a roadhouse about five miles out of town. It's always nice and quiet during the week.'

'Sounds just what I need,' he said, and pulled on his trench-coat.

He opened the door and stood to one side to let her pass. She paused in front of him, a strange expression on her face, and lightly touched the bulge under his jacket that was the butt of his Luger. 'Do we really need that with us?'

For a moment he hesitated, and then he went back into the room and slipped the Luger under his pillow. When he returned she smiled and slipped a hand through his arm. 'Thank you,' she said simply. He locked the door and they went downstairs.

Visibility was still very bad, and she drove slowly and carefully on the road out of town. The car was a small coupé and far from new, but the engine pulled well; and when they had climbed the hill out of the valley in which the town lay, the fog was thinner and visibility much improved.

The red glow from a neon sign indicated the roadhouse long before they reached it. It was a low, rambling building with, a large car park at one side, and Laura Faulkner turned the car through the gates and halted. 'What about the dog?' Shane asked.

She smiled. 'I'll leave him in the car. We can't stay long anyway. I've got to be back home no later than midnight.'

There were no more than a dozen couples dancing on the small floor when they went inside. A waiter showed them to a corner table, and Shane ordered two Martinis. When the drinks came he gave the girl a cigarette and sighed. 'This is nice. Very nice. It's a hell of a long time since I last did anything like this.'

She gently slid one of her hands over his. 'You look tired.'

He nodded. 'I've had a hard day.'

A shadow passed across her face. 'Have you – have you seen anybody?'

He grinned. 'Seen anybody? I've seen them all.'

Her eyes widened and a look of incredulity appeared on her face. After a short pause she said slowly, 'Are you going to tell me about it?'

He shrugged. 'I don't see why not. Would you like another drink?' She shook her head and he leaned back against the padded wall and started to speak.

He told her about Charles Graham, and then moved on through the events of the day, ending with an account of his second meeting with Crowther. The one thing he omitted was any reference to the footsteps.

When he had finished she sat quietly for some time gazing down into her drink, and then she said slowly, 'I don't see where it's got you. You've spoken to all three suspects. It's got to be one of them, and yet you're no further forward. Can you honestly say you suspect one of them more than the others?'

He sighed and shook his head. 'No, I can't say that I do. At first I thought I could cross Crowther off my list, but now I'm far from sure. He's too eager for me to stop the whole business. Wilby was definitely frightened, but for some reason I got the impression he was frightened of something else.'

'And Steele?' she said.

He shrugged. 'Steele is the most likely one, and not only because he's unscrupulous. He's completely self-centred. The sort of man who will always do only those things which directly benefit himself.'

'And what do you intend to do now?' she asked. 'You seem to be at a dead end.'

He frowned slightly. 'I'm not so sure. I know it looks like it, but I've got a hunch about Joe Wilby. Somehow he's the key to this whole business. If he isn't the guilty man himself, I swear he knows who is. Coming right down to it, I think Reggie Steele's my man.'

They sat there in silence, and then the band began to play an old pre-war number, with love and laughter and tender sadness in every line of it. 'Would you care to dance?' he said. She nodded, a slight smile on her lips, and they moved out on to the floor.

They danced well together, and she fitted perfectly into his arms, her dark head pressed against his shoulder. That faint, delicate perfume rose from her hair, and he was acutely aware of the soft contours of her body pressed against him.

When the band stopped playing she looked up at him, a strange-expression on her face. 'I'm sorry, Martin. I'll have to go now.' He nodded gently without speaking, and raised a hand to the waiter.

As she turned the car out of the car park into the main road, she said abruptly, 'I've been thinking I'd like to do a portrait of you. Have you got time to come up to the house tomorrow afternoon? I'd like a pencil sketch to be going on with.'

'What for – posterity?' he said lightly. She didn't reply, and they drove the rest of the way into town in silence.

When they stopped outside the hotel, she kept the engine running. 'I'm afraid I'll have to hurry,' she said. 'What about tomorrow? Can you make it?'

He nodded. 'I'll be there sometime after lunch.'

There was a moment of silence as they looked at each other, and then he turned to open the door. As his hand touched the handle she said in a sudden broken whisper, 'Martin!'

He turned and pulled her into his arms, and her supple body melted into his and the warm mouth opened like a flower. For a moment they stayed there, and then she pushed him away, gasping for breath. When she spoke, her words were shaky and uneven. 'I must go, Martin. I'll see you tomorrow.'

He reached for her again, but she placed a hand firmly against his chest and slowly and reluctantly he opened the car door and got out.

She waved once, and then the car disappeared into the fog, and he turned and went in through the door of the hotel, the blood singing in his ears, his whole body vibrant and alive for the first time in years.

He took the stairs two at a time, and he was whistling as he unlocked his door. He moved across the room in the darkness and switched on the bedside lamp, and as the shadows reached out towards him from the four corners of the room his spirits suddenly dropped.

He pulled his canvas grip out of the wardrobe and took out the half-bottle of whisky and held it to his lips. As the liquor burned its way down his throat he sat on the edge of the bed and casually slid a hand under the pillow.

A sudden frown appeared on his face, and he jumped to his feet and pulled the pillow from the bed. But he was wasting his time. The Luger had gone.

9

He made a quick check on the rest of his belongings, but they were all intact. There were no obvious signs of an intruder and the lock on the door had not been tampered with. A key had been used – that much was obvious.

For a moment he considered questioning the night porter, but he dismissed the idea. If the man had allowed someone access to the room he would certainly deny it, and no good would be served by a scene. Only two of the people he had talked to that day knew he had a gun. The first was Laura Faulkner, and the idea that she might have had anything to do with it was absurd.

That left Reggie Steele, and a sudden cold anger flared in Shane. He sat there for a moment or two longer, thinking about it, and then he got to his feet, switched off the light and left his room, locking the door behind him.

The night porter was snoring gently in an easy-chair in the corner of the foyer when he went downstairs, and he walked quietly past him and went out into the night.

It was raining hard as he walked through the deserted streets, and the fog still restricted visibility. It was shortly after one when he reached the Garland Club, and there were still cars parked in the square outside. He walked past the entrance slowly, and moved towards a narrow alley that appeared to give access to the side of the building, and then his eyes fell on something that halted him in his tracks. Laura Faulkner's car was parked at the kerb a few feet away from him.

At first he thought he was mistaken, and he approached the car to examine it more closely. A low growl caused him to move back hastily as the Dobermann poked its head through the half-open window.

He stood looking at the car, a hundred thoughts racing through his brain, and then steps sounded behind him and a gay voice said, 'Hallo, hand-some! You wouldn't be waiting for me by any chance?'

As he turned, Jenny Green emerged from the alley. In the sickly yellow light of the street lamp she looked pale and drawn, and there were dark smudges under her eyes.

As she came nearer a frown replaced her smile.

'You don't look too good,' she said. 'Is anything the matter?'

He forced a smile. 'I could do with about a week in bed, that's all. If it comes to that, you don't look so marvellous yourself.'

She shrugged. 'Three shows a night in this dump sends me home with energy for nothing but bed.' She sighed heavily. 'It can really interfere with a girl's fun.'

He smiled tightly. 'I don't seem to have much time for fun these days.'

She moved closer and put a hand on his arm. There was concern in her eyes when she looked up into his face. 'You're all tightened up inside like a spring. You'd better start unwinding fast or you'll find yourself in real trouble.'

He smiled down at her. 'You're a good kid, Jenny, but I'm short on time for what I have to do.'

She started to turn away and hesitated. 'My place is only twenty minutes' walk from here,' she said diffidently. 'I make good coffee.'

Before he could reply, the door in the alley at the side of the Garland Club opened and someone came out. Shane grabbed the girl by the arm and rushed her into the darkness of a near-by doorway. She started to protest, and he pulled her close, one arm around her shoulders.

She chuckled deep down in her throat and pressed her soft young body against him. 'Now I call this a real improvement,' she said, and Shane gently laid a finger across her lips as two people emerged from the alley.

His eyes burned out of the darkness as Laura Faulkner and Steele crossed the pavement to her car. She stood with one hand through the open window, fondling the dog's muzzle, and Steele talked to her in a low voice. Once he laughed and laid a hand on her arm in a familiar manner, and then she got into her car and drove away.

Steele started along the pavement, passing the doorway in which Shane and the girl were standing. Shane pulled her close, hiding his face against her, and Steele gave them a casual glance and moved on.

Shane stepped out of the doorway and watched him turn the corner, and there was bitterness in his eyes. From behind him Jenny said, 'Now what was all that supposed to be about? Are you interested in her, too?'

He turned quickly, a frown on his face. 'You've seen her before?'

She nodded. 'She's been visiting him at the club ever since I've worked here, and that's almost two years now.'

He started to walk along the street, hands thrust deep into his pockets. His face was like a mask, the skin drawn so tightly over the bones that in the pale light of the street lamps it resembled a skull, and there was a cold, killing rage in his heart.

Laura Faulkner had made a fool of him. She had visited him earlier in the evening for one reason only. To get him out of his room to give Steele, or one of his henchmen, a chance to look for the gun. The most damning thing of all was the fact that she herself had suggested that he leave the Luger behind. The whole thing had been cleverly planned from beginning to end. They'd banked on the fact that he'd ask her to go for a drink. If he hadn't, she would have probably suggested it herself.

He paused on the corner, debating his next move, and then suddenly he felt tired. More tired than he had felt in a long time. Laura Faulkner could wait until their appointment. He sighed deeply. At least one good thing had come out of it. He now knew for certain that something was being concealed from him. What it was he didn't know, but that could wait until the following afternoon.

He started to move forward, and Jenny Green said, 'Hey, what about me?'

He turned, surprised to find she was still there, and then a slow smile came to his face. 'Didn't you say something about coffee?' he said.

She grinned and slipped a hand inside his arm, and together they turned out of the square and walked towards the main road.

She lived in a street at the back of the university,

Jack Higgins

lined with old, brownstone houses, each with a narrow strip of garden running down to the road. Her flat was on the top floor, and when she opened the door and switched on the light he found himself in a large, comfortable living-room.

She kicked off her shoes and smiled at him, an expression of relief on her face. 'I must wash my face and change into something comfortable,' she said. 'Make yourself at home. I'll only be a minute.'

He wandered about the room, examining things. Through the half-open door of the bedroom he caught a glimpse of her standing in front of a mirror unfastening her stockings, and the contours of her supple body stood out boldly under her nylon slip.

He turned away quickly, his throat dry, and sat down in a chair by the fire-place. When he picked up a magazine his hands were shaking slightly, and his breathing was ragged and uneven. Somewhere he could hear water running as a tap was turned on. A few minutes later she walked into the room, pinning her hair up at the back of her head.

She was wearing an old quilted dressing-gown and furlined slippers. Her face was scrubbed clean, and without her make-up she looked startlingly young and innocent.

She went into the kitchen and filled the kettle. Shane lit a cigarette and went and leaned in the doorway, and there was puzzlement in his voice. 'How the hell did you get mixed up in this sort of life?' he said.

She turned, suddenly serious. 'Don't get any wrong ideas. I'm in show business – not the other thing. Anyone who gets invited up here gets asked because I like him and for no other reason.'

He smiled gently. 'I'm sorry if I spoke out of turn.' She started to spoon coffee into a jug, and he went on. 'How did you come to work for Steele?'

She carried the coffee into the living-room on a tray, and he followed her. 'It was the old story. All my life I wanted to be an actress. I was raised, if you can call it that, in a Manchester slum. I went to London when I was seventeen, got a job in a shop during the day, and enrolled as a student at evening classes in a third-rate drama academy.'

'It sounds like a bad plot,' Shane told her.

She nodded. 'Finally, I thought I knew enough to get a job in the theatre. I haunted the agencies for nearly three months and was handed just about every proposition under the sun – all of the same kind, naturally. Finally I managed to get a job as a dancer in a cheap touring revue.'

Shane grinned. 'Red-nosed comedians and strip I suppose.'

She nodded. 'It folded in Burnham, and Reggie Steele offered me a job.'

'With no strings attached?' he said.

She shrugged, and handed him his coffee. 'He had a passing fancy for me at first, but it didn't last. It never does with him.'

He gave her a cigarette, and they sat in silence for several minutes. She rested her head against the back of the chair and closed her eyes, and Shane stretched out his legs and tried to relax.

It was impossible. Her dressing-gown had fallen slightly open and revealed the long, breath-taking sweep of thigh, and his stomach churned as he remembered how she had looked through the half-open door of the bedroom.

It had been a long time since he'd had a woman. Too long. He got to his feet and walked restlessly over to the window. A policeman passed under the lamp outside, his cape streaming with rain, and Jenny Green said quietly, 'You're in some sort of trouble, aren't you? Real trouble, I mean.'

He turned and faced her with a slight smile. 'Nothing I can't handle.'

She nodded slowly. 'You look the kind of man who could handle most things.'

There was an expression that was almost amusement in her eyes and his throat went dry. He drew a deep breath and said, 'I suppose I'd better be going. It's getting late.'

She smiled faintly. 'Must you? You can stay here. I've got plenty of room.'

He shook his head. 'Thanks for the offer, but

there might be an important message waiting for me back at my hotel.'

She moved very close to him and looked up into his face. 'I saw you in the mirror watching me undress.'

He clenched his hands and tried to keep his voice steady. 'I just happened to be passing the door.'

She chuckled deep down in her throat. 'Why do you think I left the door open?'

His palms were moist, and in his stomach a knot slowly hardened. When he gripped her arms, his hands were trembling. 'It's been a long time, Jenny. A hell of a long time.'

She reached up on tiptoe and gently kissed him on the mouth. 'Give me two minutes,' she said and disappeared into the bedroom.

He stood gazing into space for a moment, and then he picked up his trench-coat and walked to the door. As he started to open it she called softly to him. He hesitated for a moment, and then, with a smothered curse, threw down his coat and crossed to the bedroom in three quick strides.

For a moment, as he stood in the doorway, he caught a breath-taking glimpse of her lying there waiting for him, and then she switched off the lamp and laughed softly at him from the darkness.

10

He awoke shortly after dawn. Rain had drifted in through the partly opened window during the night, and damp curtains flapped listlessly in a slight breeze. The girl was sleeping, head turned slightly away from him, black hair spread across the pillow. He felt completely relaxed and content, and after a while he drifted into sleep again.

When he next awoke he was alone. There was a note on the pillow to say that she'd gone to the club for the lunch-time show. He glanced at his watch. It was almost twelve-thirty and he swore softly, remembering his appointment with Laura Faulkner.

He dressed quickly, and then went into the kitchen and snatched a hasty breakfast of coffee and toast. Twenty minutes later he left the flat and walked briskly into the centre of the town until he came to a taxi rank.

The fog had lifted a little, but it was still raining steadily when he left the cab outside her house and walked towards the front door. Somehow the place looked more neglected and run down than ever, and he followed the path around to the back of the house and walked down towards her studio.

He mounted the steps, and as he paused outside the door the Dobermann growled. He opened the door and stepped inside.

She was working at the easel, a look of concentration on her face, and as he entered she blushed like a young girl, as if remembering how they had parted the previous night.

'Hallo, Martin,' she said. 'I'm glad you could come.'

She was wearing the tartan trews and the Spanish shirt knotted at her waist, and it came to him, almost with a sense of wonder, that she was beautiful.

When he spoke his voice sounded calm and easy. 'I almost didn't make it. I overslept.'

She raised her eyebrows slightly. 'Didn't you go to bed when I left you?'

He lit a cigarette and said calmly, 'As a matter of fact I had rather an unsettling night. When I got back to my room I found I'd had a visitor.'

Her eyes were suddenly wary, but she kept her gaze studiously on the painting. 'And who was that?'

He moved across the room until he was standing looking over her shoulder. 'Whoever it was, took my Luger. I sat down and thought about it real hard, and I remembered that only two people knew I had it. You and Reggie Steele. It couldn't possibly have been you, so I decided I'd better have a word with Reggie.'

Her voice was still calm, but her hand shook slightly when she dipped her brush into the paint. 'And what did he have to say?'

Shane shook his head and said softly, 'I didn't get a chance to talk to him. He was deeply engaged in conversation with someone else when I got there.'

There was a moment of silence, and she still kept on painting. Sudden anger lifted inside Shane, and he grabbed her by the shoulder and spun her round. 'You told me you'd never met Reggie Steele,' he said, his fingers biting into her flesh. 'You lied to me. I want to know why.'

There was a sudden, frenzied growling as the Dobermann hurled itself across the room. As Shane released her, Laura Faulkner grabbed for the dog's collar, pulling it back. She leaned down and spoke softly into its ear, her hands gently fondling its ears, and after a while it retreated to the divan and lay down again, its black eyes fixed unwinkingly on Shane.

When she turned, her cheeks were flushed and

there was anger in her eyes. She took out a cigarette and lit it with shaking fingers, and when she spoke there was a slight tremble in her voice. 'If you try to lay a hand on me again I'll let the dog tear your throat out, and believe me – he can do it.'

Shane moved back until he was leaning against the wall. When he spoke, his voice was level and calm. 'All right, let's cut the dramatics and get down to some hard fact. When I first spoke to you, you told me you'd never met any of the men who'd known your brother in Korea. Last night I saw you coming out of the Garland Club with Reggie Steele, and from what I've been told you've been visiting him there regularly for years.'

She took a few nervous paces away from him, and when she turned there was real anger in her eyes. 'All right. You've asked for some hard facts – I'll give you some.'

She untied the knot at her waist, pulled the blouse from her body with one fluid motion, and stood facing him. 'Now don't start getting any silly ideas just because I'm treating you like an adult.'

She was wearing no brassière and her breasts were superb, full and ripe, with delicate nipples. A sudden dryness clutched Shane by the throat, and then he saw the scar and sucked in his breath. It started beneath her left breast and ran up into her shoulder, a jagged line of white showing clearly against her tanned skin.

He swallowed hard. 'Who did it?'

She quickly pulled on the blouse and knotted it again at her waist. 'My loving brother Simon,' she said. 'Or step-brother, I should say, because that's what he really was.'

Shane shook his head in bewilderment. 'Simon?' he said. 'But I don't understand.'

'It's easy. When he was drunk he was capable of anything. One night he tried to get fresh with me. We struggled, knocked over a table with some liquor bottles on it, and I fell on one of the broken bottles.'

'And what did your father have to say about it?' Shane said.

She shrugged. 'My father thought the sun shone out of him. Who was I to disillusion him? I told him it was an accident. That we'd just been fooling around. The only good thing that came out of it was that Simon left me strictly alone after that.'

'He was always wild,' Shane said, 'but I never thought he was as bad as that.'

She laughed tightly. 'Oh, there's worse to come. After my father's stroke, Simon took control of the firm. For two years he spent money like water – other people's money. The day he met you in that bar he was just one step ahead of the law. The accountants were due the following week, and he was in too deep to be able to cover it up.'

Shane's eyes narrowed. 'So that's why he volunteered for Korea?'

She nodded. 'It was rather clever really. The last place the police would think of looking. We had no idea where he was until we received news of his death from the War Office.'

Shane sighed. 'He certainly paid the bill in full at the end.'

She threw back her head and laughed harshly. 'You think so, do you? As far as I'm concerned he could never pay. My father had a second stroke when he heard. It's left him in the state he's in today. It took almost every penny we had in the world to make good those losses to the firm.' She turned and added bitterly, 'Perhaps you've noticed the condition of the house and grounds.'

He nodded and said slowly, 'This is all very interesting, and it tells me things about Simon I never knew, but he's dead and buried now. What has it got to do with you and Reggie Steele?'

She moved to the window and spoke without looking at him. 'He came to see us when he'd been back from Korea for about six months. It was just after he opened his first club. I'd been so wrapped up in looking after father I hadn't had time for men. He paid a great deal of attention to me, and I rather lost my head. He can be very charming, you know.'

'I don't doubt it,' Shane said drily.

She didn't seem to notice his remark. 'I wrote some rather indiscreet letters to him during our affair. I finally realized what a swine he was and tried to break things off. He asked me to go down to his office. He produced the letters and sealed them in an envelope which he addressed to my father. He's been holding them over my head ever since.'

'And what's his price?' Shane said.

She coloured slightly. 'I'm on call when he wants me.'

Shane's hands clenched and he swore softly. 'The lousy bastard.'

She fumbled for another cigarette. 'It isn't as bad as it sounds. Sometimes he forgets about me for months at a time, but then he remembers and I get a phone call.'

'Haven't you ever considered going to the police?'

She shook her head. 'That's the one thing I dare not do. My father has his lucid moments – times when he's completely normal. The shock of another scandal would kill him. I'm not going to risk that.'

There was a moment's silence, and then Shane said slowly, 'What about last night? Did he ask you to get me out of my hotel room?'

She moved close to him, her face grave, and laid a hand on his arm. 'I didn't have anything to do with that. If Reggie stole the gun, then he did so without telling me.'

'Then why *did* you visit me last night?'

A slow blush spread across her face, and she dropped her gaze. 'I meant what I said,' she told him. 'I was worried about you.'

He slipped a hand under her chin and tilted her face until he was looking directly into the amber eyes. 'I'm sorry.' He smiled briefly. 'For what I thought and for what I said.' He turned away from her and walked to the door.

As he opened it she said in a worried voice, 'Martin – what are you going to do now?'

His face was expressionless. 'I think I'll have a long talk with Steele,' he said. 'Perhaps I can help him to see the error of his ways.' He closed the door as an expression of shocked dismay appeared on her face, and walked away before she could protest.

He caught a bus into town and went straight to his hotel. As he entered the dingy foyer, the young receptionist was standing in front of a large mirror on the wall, adjusting a stocking. She hurriedly pulled down her skirt and glanced round.

A smile appeared on her face, and she tried to look coy. 'I'll have to be more careful in future,' she said as she went behind the reception desk and took down his key.

She was wearing an expensive gaberdine suit and had obviously just been to the hairdresser's. Shane grinned as he took his key from her. 'You must have come into a fortune.'

She raised her arms and turned, slowly. 'Like it?'

He nodded. 'I certainly do, but it must have cost a packet.'

She shrugged and a cunning expression appeared in her eyes. 'That's what comes of having the right kind of boy friend.'

He started to turn away, and she made a sudden exclamation. 'I knew there was something. The night porter took a message for you last night. He told me to let him know when you came in. He said it was important. I'll tell him to come up to your room.'

Shane hesitated, a slight frown on his face, but she had already lifted the house phone and was dialling a number. He shrugged and went slowly upstairs, wondering who could have been trying to get in touch with him.

It was quiet in his room, and somehow the events of the previous night seemed unreal and far off. He took a clean shirt from his grip and started to change, and a moment later there was a knock on the door and the night porter entered.

'I understand you've got a message for me,' Shane said.

The porter nodded. 'There was a phone call, sir. Just after midnight. I tried putting it through to your room, but couldn't get a reply. When I came upstairs, you weren't here.'

Shane nodded. 'Who was the message from?'

The porter took out a small red notebook and thumbed through the pages. After a moment he gave a grunt of satisfaction. 'I've got it here, sir. The gentleman's name was Wilby. He said you'd know who he was.'

Shane took a deep breath to steady his voice, and said calmly, 'What did he want?'

The porter frowned. 'It didn't make much sense to me, sir. He said I'd to tell you that if you wanted the answer to the question you asked him, you'd better go and see him.'

Shane stared at his reflection in the wardrobe mirror, a slight frown on his face. After a few moments the porter coughed. 'Will there be anything else, sir?'

Shane shook his head and said slowly. 'If I want anything I'll ring.'

As the door closed softly behind him, he turned and walked across to the window. For some peculiar reason he felt depressed and uneasy. It was almost as if he didn't want to hear what Wilby had to tell him.

There was a little whisky left in the bottle, and he drank it slowly and then finished dressing. As he was reaching for his jacket there was a quiet knock on the door.

When he opened it he found a tall, slightly built young man in a belted raincoat and slouch hat standing there. A slight smile illuminated the lean, aquiline face. 'Mr Shane?' he said. 'Mr Martin Shane?'

Shane nodded, his eyes wary. 'That's right. What can I do for you?'

The man smiled pleasantly. 'My name's Lomax – Detective Inspector – Burnham C.I.D. I wonder if I could have a few words with you?'

He moved into the room, and Shane closed the door and turned to face him. 'I'm afraid I haven't got a great deal of time to spare, Inspector,' he said. 'What was it you wanted to see me about?'

Lomax produced a briar pipe and held a match to it. When it was drawing to his satisfaction he glanced up. There was a smile on his face, but his eyes were cold and businesslike. 'Did you know a man called Wilby, Mr Shane?'

Shane frowned, suddenly on guard. 'Joe Wilby, you mean? Yes, I was in Korea with him.' Lomax still looked at him steadily, the slight fixed smile on his mouth, and Shane said angrily, 'Look here, what is this?'

Lomax pushed his hat to the back of his head and said calmly. 'Joe Wilby stuck his head in the gas-oven early this morning. His wife spent the night with friends. She only found him an hour ago.'

Shane took a deep breath and reached for a cigarette. 'And what's it got to do with me?' he said calmly.

Lomax frowned and examined the bowl of his pipe. 'Wilby's wife seems to think that you've had something to do with her husband's death, Mr Shane,' he said gently. 'I wonder if you'd mind coming down to the station with me? I'd like you to make a statement.'

11

The inquest was held on the following morning, and afterwards Shane went back to the hotel, his mind a prey to conflicting emotions. He sat on the bed and stared out of the window at the driving rain, thinking about what had happened. After a while there was a knock on the door and Lomax came in.

He stood at the end of the bed, lighting his pipe, and his face was grave. Shane looked up and said sourly. 'What the hell do you want? The coroner said all there was to be said.'

Lomax shook his head. 'I'm afraid not, Shane. I know he gave you a rough time, but we've got to face facts. There seems to be no doubt that Wilby committed suicide for one reason only. He was afraid of you. He felt that you were hounding him because of what happened in Korea. The note he left proves that.'

Shane got to his feet and walked to the window. 'Let's get to the point, Inspector. I've got things to do.'

'Not in this town,' Lomax said evenly.

There was a moment of silence, and Shane turned slowly and looked at him. 'What's that supposed to mean?'

Lomax shrugged. 'I've found out a lot about you since yesterday afternoon. I know what happened to you in Korea, and I know where you've been for the past six or seven years. You've had a rough break, but that doesn't alter the facts.'

'And just what are the facts as you see them?' Shane said.

Lomax frowned and there was a serious expression on his face. 'This obsession of yours has caused too much trouble as it is. I think you ought to catch a train for London this afternoon. Maybe you should enter that hospital now.'

Shane shook his head. 'Nothing doing,' he said definitely. 'For me that hospital is the end of the line. I've still got a few more days coming to me.'

'Not in this town,' repeated Lomax firmly.

Shane smiled grimly. 'You can't run me out and you know it.'

'Can't I?' Lomax said gently. 'You've just spent six years in an institution. What would happen if I got the superintendent on the phone and told him you were a danger to yourself and those around you?'

Shane took a quick step towards him, his face contorted with rage, and Lomax shook his head. 'Now don't try anything silly. It won't get you anywhere.' He walked to the door and opened it. When he turned, there was pity on his face. 'I'm sorry about this, Shane. As I said before, you've had a rough break, but if you're not on that train this afternoon I'll have to make that phone call.' The door closed gently and he was gone.

Shane stood in the centre of the room for several minutes staring at the door, and then he went into the bathroom and swilled cold water over his face. His temples were throbbing and there was a slight ache behind one eye. He took two of his pills and went into the bedroom and packed his grip. Five minutes later he went downstairs and asked for his bill at the desk.

It was raining hard when he left the hotel, and he took a cab from the rank at the end of the street and told the driver to take him to Charles Graham's house.

As he walked up the drive towards the house the last traces of fog disappeared, shredded by the heavy rain, but his headache was still there. He pressed the button of the bell firmly, and almost immediately the door was opened by Graham himself.

Jack Higgins

'Come in, Shane! Come in!' he said. 'I saw you coming along the drive. I'm having to manage without Mrs Grimshaw today. I'm afraid she's caught a cold.'

He took Shane's coat and put it in a small cloakroom at the side of the hall, and then led the way upstairs to the conservatory. They sat in basket-chairs, and Graham gave him a cigarette.

There was a moment of silence before Shane said, 'I suppose you've read about Wilby in the papers?'

Graham's face registered no change of expression. 'I read the brief announcement of his suicide in last night's paper, but nothing more.'

Shane leaned back in the chair and stared up through the glass roof into the leaden sky. 'He left a note in which he said I'd been hounding him because of what happened in Korea. He said he couldn't stand it any longer.'

'And had you been hounding him?' Graham said gently.

Shane sighed. 'I suppose you could call it that. I had a talk with him at his home the day before yesterday. I told him I meant business. He was scared to death. He even paid someone to beat me up.'

'Has the inquest been held yet?' Graham asked.

Shane nodded. 'Ten o'clock this morning, and the coroner made no bones about laying the blame

134

squarely on me. I've even had a warning from the police to get out of town.'

'And are you going?'

Shane shook his head. 'That's why I'm here. I've left my hotel to put them off the scent, but I need time to work this thing out. I wondered if I might stay here.'

'Do you think that would be wise?' Graham said. 'After all, what is there to stay for? Surely the whole thing's settled now that Wilby's dead.'

Shane got to his feet and moved over to the window. 'Not in my book it isn't. When Wilby spoke to me the other night he was frightened, but it wasn't just because of me. There was another greater reason, I'm sure of that.'

'You mean you don't think he committed suicide?'

Shane turned and looked at him. 'According to the coroner's report he was drunk when he put his head in that oven. Perhaps he was put in.'

Graham shook his head. 'It won't do, Martin. It won't do at all. I think the police are right. You should leave.'

'I couldn't even if I wanted to,' Shane told him. 'I've another reason for staying now. It concerns Simon Faulkner's sister. She made a bit of a fool of herself over Steele a few years ago. Wrote him some rather indiscreet letters, and he's been blackmailing her ever since.'

Graham sat up with a start. 'Are you absolutely sure about that?'

Shane nodded. 'So sure that I intend to get those letters out of him if I have to break his bloody neck doing it.'

Graham shook his head slowly. 'That may turn out to be more difficult than you imagine. You can hardly expect Steele to hand them over without a murmur.'

'I think I can manage to persuade him,' Shane said. He crushed his cigarette in an ashtray and took a deep breath. 'Well, what about it, Graham? Can I stay here for a while?'

Graham sighed deeply and got to his feet. 'I'm afraid not, Martin. I think Laura Faulkner should put this blackmailing business in the hands of the police, and I think you should get out. It's the only thing to do under the circumstances.'

Shane shrugged and said calmly, 'Fair enough, Graham. You've made your point.'

As they walked through the conservatory to the door Graham said, 'You'll leave town, then?'

Shane shook his head. 'Nothing doing. I've got another contact in Burnham – a dancer at Steele's club called Jenny Green. I'll have to see if she can do anything for me.'

Graham sighed and shrugged his shoulders helplessly. 'Well, I've done my best.' He got Shane's coat, and they moved out on to the porch together and stood at the top of the steps. Shane turned to him and held out his hand. 'I don't suppose I'll be seeing you again.'

Graham placed a hand on his shoulder. 'It's not a very pleasant world we live in at times, is it? You and I, more than most men, have good cause to know that.' He turned abruptly and went back inside, and Shane walked away slowly, a slight frown on his face.

He walked down to the main road, and went into the first telephone box he came to and phoned Jenny Green at the flat. There was no reply, and after a second unsuccessful attempt he tried the Garland Club.

He waited in an agony of impatience, and when her voice sounded clearly over the wire he slumped against the side of the booth in relief. 'Martin Shane here,' he said. 'I've got to see you, Jenny.'

There was immediate anxiety in her voice. 'What's happened? Is everything all right?'

He tried to sound unconcerned. 'Nothing serious. As a matter of fact I'm in a bit of a jam and I was wondering if you could help. I need somewhere to stay for a couple of days.'

She chuckled. 'If that's all that's worrying you, don't give it a second thought. You can stay at my place.'

'That's grand,' he said. 'But how do I get in?'

Someone shouted something to her, and he could

hear music start up in the background. She said hastily, 'I've got a show now. I'll have to go. There's a spare key under the carpet outside the front door. Make yourself comfortable and I'll get there as soon as I can.'

She murmured a hurried good-bye and replaced the receiver. Suddenly Shane felt tired – really tired all the way through, and he quickly phoned for a cab and waited for it outside the booth, taking deep breaths of the rain-washed air to steady himself.

When the cab came he gave the driver Jenny's address and slumped back against the cushioned seat. The journey took only ten minutes, and he paid off the driver quickly and hurried up the path to the house.

He found the key under the carpet as she had said, and in a moment was in the quiet safety of the flat. He dropped his canvas grip on to the floor, and went into the kitchen. He found a bottle of cooking sherry in a cupboard, and swallowed a large glassful, wretching at the bitter taste, and then he went into the bedroom.

The pain in his head was worse – much worse. He took two more pills and lay on the bed, a pillow behind his head.

He started to go over the events of the past few days, but they didn't seem to have any connexion or fit together into a comprehensible pattern.

He had an uneasy feeling that he had overlooked a vital point. Something which would make sense of the whole business. He was still thinking about it as he drifted into sleep.

When he awoke it was quite dark. The pain in his head had gone, and he lay on the bed for a few moments, staring at the pale oblong of the window, before swinging his legs down to the floor.

He opened the door and went into the living-room. At that moment Jenny emerged from the kitchen, a tray in her hands. When she saw him she smiled gaily. 'I was just going to call you.'

Shane ran his fingers through his hair and looked at his watch. It was almost seven o'clock and he swore softly. 'I didn't realize it was so late.'

She passed him a cup of coffee. 'Whatever you've got to do can wait.'

He shook his head firmly. 'I'm afraid it can't. What time does Steele usually visit Club Eight?'

She frowned. 'Seven o'clock. Sometimes a little later. Why?'

He ignored her question. 'How long does he stay there?'

She shrugged. 'I don't really know – perhaps an hour. He checks the previous night's receipts with the manager.'

Shane glanced at his watch and nodded in satisfaction. 'That gives me all the time in the world.' He went into the bedroom and got his coat.

When he returned she was pacing nervously up and down in front of the fire-place, a cigarette between her fingers. She turned sharply and there was anxiety on her face. 'I've minded my own business up to now, Martin,' she said. 'But you've got me worried. What are you up to?'

He slipped an arm about her waist and kissed her on the mouth. He moved to the door. 'With any luck I should be back before you leave for the show.' She took one quick step towards him, but the door closed and he was gone before she could protest.

When he arrived at the Garland Club there were still faint traces of fog in the air and a steady rain hammered into the pavement. There was a light in the foyer, and as he walked past he saw the doorman busily mopping the floor.

It was quiet in the alley at the side of the building, and he opened the staff door and stepped inside. A narrow passage stretched before him, and he could hear the cheerful clatter of the kitchens. There was a stairway on his left, and he mounted it quietly.

He found himself standing at the end of the corridor leading to Steele's office. The dressing-rooms were quiet as he passed them, and the far end of the corridor was shrouded in darkness.

He stood outside Steele's office and listened intently, but there was no sound. After a moment he tried to open the door, but it was locked. There was another door a few feet away down the turning of the corridor. It opened easily to his touch, and when he switched on the light he found himself in a lavatory.

There was a narrow, frosted-glass window in the far wall, and he opened it and looked out on to a lead-covered flat roof. He switched off the light, and then eased himself out through the window and dropped down on to the roof.

He approached the window of Steele's office and gave a grunt of satisfaction as he saw that it was ajar. He slipped a hand through the narrow opening, unhooked the catch inside, and threw a leg over the window-sill.

He paused, his eyes probing the darkness, and a voice said, 'Hallo, old man. I've been expecting you to call again.' The light flicked on, momentarily blinding him, and Steele was standing by the door, a slight smile on his face.

Shane started to move, his fists raised, and then something exploded on the back of his head, flooding him with agony, and the floor lifted to meet him.

There was a great roaring in his ears, and through it he heard Steele say, 'Make it look good, Frenchy. Fill him up with whisky and then dump him on the railway line at the back of Market Street. When they find what's left of him, they'll think he got drunk trying to drown his sorrows and wandered down there in the dark. I'll be at Hampton if you need me.'

Shane groaned and Steele dropped to one knee and grinned. 'Don't worry, old man,' he said genially, 'you won't feel a thing.'

Shane summoned up everything he'd got, and spat in Steele's face. Steele gave a smothered exclamation and got to his feet. He wiped his face with a handkerchief, and smiled viciously. 'I always did hate your guts, you bastard.' His foot lifted suddenly into the side of Shane's neck, and he cried out in agony and plunged into darkness.

12

Something was burning its way into his throat, and he choked and tried to struggle, but a hand pushed solidly against his chest and he fell back, his head striking a wall.

He opened his eyes and focused on a face. He frowned, trying to remember where he was, and a voice said, 'Maybe you hit him too hard, Frenchy?'

Frenchy grunted. 'So what? He's going anyway, isn't he?'

He took a firm grip of Shane's coat and lifted him into a sitting position. He grinned evilly. 'O.K., Jack. Drink your medicine like a good boy.'

The neck of a bottle was rammed between Shane's teeth, and whisky gurgled into his throat. A terrible nausea flooded through him. His body jerked convulsively and vomit erupted from his mouth in a fine spray.

Frenchy jumped up with a curse and kicked him viciously in the body. 'The bastard's ruined my coat,' he snarled. 'I'll never get the stink of this stuff off.' He hurled the bottle against a wall with a crash, and moved away. 'I'm going for another bottle. When Joe arrives with the car, put laughing boy here in the back and wait for me.' A door banged and he was gone.

It was quiet except for the steady sizzle of the rain, and Shane opened his eyes cautiously and looked around him. He was lying in a cobbled yard, and there was a man in a raincoat standing a few feet away from him facing a door. He decided he must be somewhere at the rear of the Garland Club.

He felt terrible. His head was splitting and there was a feeling of nausea in his stomach as if he were going to be sick again at any moment. He was utterly exhausted and all the strength seemed to have been drained out of him, and yet he knew that he was in deadly danger. If he were still here when Frenchy returned it was curtains and nothing on earth could save him.

The man by the door took out a packet of cigarettes and put one in his mouth. At that moment Shane's hand closed over a loose cobblestone, and he dug his fingers desperately into the ground and pulled. The stone came free so suddenly that he rocked back against the wall. He took a deep breath and pushed himself upright.

The man by the door struck a match and cupped it in his hands against the wind. He leaned over and Shane staggered forward and smashed the cobblestone into the back of the exposed neck. As the man keeled over, Shane lurched across the yard and out through a narrow opening.

He found himself in the alley at the side of the club and as a sudden outcry broke out behind him, he emerged into the square. He moved along the pavement at a shambling trot and turned into the first side street he came to. He finally stopped from sheer exhaustion after turning and twisting through a maze of back streets for ten or fifteen minutes. He moved inside the gate of a scrap yard and sank down on his knees in the shadows. His stomach seemed to move and then he gagged suddenly.

It was some time before he could think clearly again. He cleaned himself up as far as he was able and lit a cigarette with hands that shook violently. He felt detached from his surroundings and as he started to walk, the buildings around him seemed to float in the thin fog and heavy rain.

There was a dull ache in the side of his neck where Steele had kicked him and his head seemed to swell like a balloon and coloured lights burst around him in the darkness. He paused and hung on to a lamp-post, letting the rain fall on his upturned face and after a while he felt better.

He took over half an hour to walk back to the flat and when he reached it there was a black saloon car parked outside. He stood by the gate and looked at the car, a slight frown on his face and then he entered the front door and mounted the stairs quietly.

As he moved towards the door there was a faint cry of pain that sounded somehow remote and far away. Shane stood there listening for a moment and then he moved quietly along to the end of the passage and opened the landing window.

An ornamental ledge a foot wide ran along the face of the building about three feet beneath the windows. He quickly scrambled out on to the ledge and started to edge his way along to the living-room window.

The rain hammered against his face and every muscle in his body seemed to tremble as he moved forward and peered round the edge of the window into the living-room.

A man in a dirty brown raincoat stood by the door, his arms folded impassively, no expression on his wooden face. Jenny Green was crouched on the floor by the fire-place, a dazed look on her tear-stained face. She was wearing a pair of black panties and the rest of her clothes were scattered about the room.

Frenchy was sitting in a chair beside her, heating a poker in the fire. There was an evil smile on his face and he reached out and nudged her with the toe of his shoe and said something. She shook her head vehemently and he slapped her across the face.

Shane moved along the ledge towards the bedroom window, black rage erupting inside him. He remembered that Jenny had left the window slightly open at the bottom on the night he had spent with her and prayed that it was her usual custom.

He slipped once and clawed desperately at the wall and then his right hand got a grip on the edge of the window and a moment later, he was holding on to the sill. His fingers found the gap he had been praying for, and he pushed up the sash silently and scrambled into the room.

There was an ornamental lamp at the side of the bed made from a French brandy bottle. He dispensed with the shade and the bulb and hefting the bottle in one hand, approached the door. He opened it quietly and peered in.

Frenchy had just taken the poker from the fire. It glowed white hot and he turned to the girl and said, 'Now start talking. I know you've been making quite a friend of this bloke Shane. All you've got to do is to tell me where he might be and I won't have to use this on you.'

The man at the door moved to get a better view and Shane stepped into the room and threw the bottle at him with all his strength. It caught the man in the side of the neck just below the right ear. He gave a strangled cry and fell back. His fingers scrabbled against the wall for a moment, and then slid to the floor and lay still.

Shane heard a cry of warning from Jenny and ducked as the poker whistled past his head. As Frenchy moved forward, Shane rammed the sofa against his legs, sending him staggering to the floor. He vaulted over the sofa and kicked savagely at the unprotected head, but Frenchy twisted desperately, grabbed him by the ankle and pulled him down on top of him.

For a few moment they rolled wildly from side to side, limbs threshing as Shane tried to get a grip on his opponent's throat, and then Frenchy shortened his arm and smashed a fist into his mouth.

Shane rolled away from him, head swimming and scrambled to his feet, putting the sofa between them. Frenchy jumped up like a cat, triumph in his eyes and moved towards him.

And then Shane was tired no longer. He felt cold and calm and filled with the killing urge that had so often saved him in Korea. As Frenchy moved in close and swung a tremendous punch at his head, Shane ducked and rammed his stiffened fingers into the other man's throat just above the Adam's Apple.

Frenchy screamed horribly and fell on the floor, writhing and choking in agony. Shane stood looking down at him with no pity in his heart and then Jenny came round the sofa in a rush and flung herself into his arms. 'Thank God!' she said. 'Thank God you came. I've never been so scared in my life.'

He held her gently in his arms for a moment and then pushed her towards the bedroom. 'You'd better get some clothes on,' he said. 'I'll get rid of these two.'

As the bedroom door closed behind her, Shane hoisted Frenchy on to his shoulders and carried him downstairs to the car. When he returned to the flat his heart was pounding and he felt slightly dizzy. He remembered there was some sherry in a cupboard in the kitchen and went and half-filled a tumbler and drank it down slowly.

After a while he felt better. The man by the door, groaned slightly and tried to sit up. Shane lit a cigarette and went into the bedroom. Jenny was sitting in front of the dressing-table, applying make-up with a hand that shook a little.

'How do you feel?' he said.

She turned with a wan smile. 'Not so good. It was like something that happens in a nightmare. I still can't quite believe it's all over.'

Shane squeezed her arm gently. 'Nobody's going to bother you any more. I promise you.' She turned back to the mirror and he went on, 'Have you any idea where Hampton is?'

She nodded. 'It's a village about nine miles out of town on the main road north.'

'What would Reggie Steele be doing there?'

She shrugged. 'That's easy. He has a place just outside Hampton on the river. Garth Cottage it's called.'

Shane nodded. 'How do I get there?'

She frowned. 'There's an hourly service from Central Bus Station. You get off at Five Lane Ends just outside the village. There's a dirt road by the bus stop. The cottage is about two hundred yards along it in some trees by the river.'

Shane looked at her in the mirror. 'You look pretty foul,' he said. 'I'd give the club a miss tonight if I were you.'

She nodded and threw down the comb she was using. 'I think I will,' she said. 'In fact I don't feel like going back to the place ever again.'

He moved behind her and placed a hand reassuringly on her shoulder. 'We'll work something out, Jenny. Don't worry.' He walked to the door. 'I've got a little business to attend to. It shouldn't take long. I'll be back as soon as I can.'

She was too tired to argue. She nodded her head dumbly at him and he closed the door gently and turned to the man he had left lying on the floor. He was on his feet, leaning against the wall, moaning softly. Shane pushed him through the door in front of him and they went downstairs together.

Frenchy was still unconscious in the back seat and Shane pushed the other man in with him and got behind the wheel and drove away. He took the car down into the centre of town and parked it in a back street near the bus station. When he looked in through the rear window, Frenchy was still out and his friend was huddled in the corner of the seat, head in hands. Shane left them there and walked quickly away.

When he reached the station, there was a bus for Hampton just leaving and he ran for it, jumping on to the platform as it turned out of the concrete loading bay. He went upstairs and sat in a front seat, smoking and thinking about Steele. Whatever happened he intended to have those letters and some answers to a few things.

It was almost nine-thirty when he dropped off the bus and walked along the dirt road Jenny had mentioned. He could see a light through the trees before he came to the cottage. It was a lonely, eerie spot and the river rushed by only a few yards away at the bottom of a short slope.

He followed a path round to the rear of the building and found a Daimler standing in the cobbled yard. There was no light in the kitchen window and he lifted the old-fashioned latch and opened the back door.

He walked quietly along a short, stone-flagged corridor. There was a light showing under the door at the far end. He hesitated, then opened it quietly and stepped inside.

13

Steele was sitting in front of a blazing fire. There was a bottle of whisky on the table at his hand and it was almost empty. He had a beautiful, double-barrelled shotgun across his knees which he was cleaning with an oily rag.

A woman was lying on the sofa and she pushed herself up and swung her legs to the floor. She had been drinking and her blouse was unbuttoned at the front. She reached for the bottle and her eyes met Shane's. Her mouth fell open and there was indignation in her voice. 'Heh, Reggie,' she cried, 'I thought you said this was going to be a private party.'

Steele looked up, a frown on his face and then he smiled. 'Hallo, Shane. What a pleasant surprise.' His eyes were glassy and he slurred his words slightly as if he were drunk.

Shane leaned against the door and lit a cigarette.

'We didn't get a chance to finish our conversation last time we met.'

Steele reached for the bottle and poured some whisky into his glass. 'How did you manage to find my little hideaway?'

Shane shrugged. 'I've got friends, which is more than I can say for you.'

Steele emptied his glass and placed it carefully on the table. 'What happened to Frenchy?'

Shane laughed grimly. 'He annoyed me,' he said. 'I don't think he'll annoy anybody for quite a while now.'

There was a short silence broken only by the sound of the raindrops as they fell down the wide chimney and hissed into the fire. Steele said in a dreamy voice, 'I'm beginning to realize we underestimated you, Shane.'

'You certainly did,' Shane said and some sixth sense made him reach back quickly and lift the latch of the door behind him.

Steele smiled pleasantly. 'I can see I'm going to have to take drastic action.' He raised the shotgun and fired one barrel.

Shane was already half-way through the door, crouching and he felt a sudden sharp pain as several stray pellets found their mark. He ran along the corridor and jumped out into the rain, Steele a few paces behind.

The gun blazed and he threw himself to the

ground, shot whistling through the air above his head. Steele called, 'I'll get you, you bastard. I've plenty more cartridges.' He didn't sound drunk any more.

Shane ran for the cover of the trees. He plunged into them as the gun roared again, lost his footing and rolled down the short slope to the river. He tried to catch at something to arrest his progress, but he was too late. He rolled over the edge of the earth bank and fell into the river with a strangled cry.

He surfaced some twenty yards downstream as the current carried him onwards in an iron hand. He allowed himself to drift with it, keeping his head above water and then his feet touched bottom. A sudden, unexpected eddy flung him against a sandbank and he staggered out of the water, clawing at the harsh tussocks of grass and dragged himself up the short slope through the trees.

He came out into the meadow and saw the lights of the cottage a hundred yards away to his right and set off towards them at a shambling run. He approached the back door cautiously and then he heard a sound behind him. It was Steele coming back from the river, the shotgun across one shoulder. Shane stood in the shadows and waited.

As Steele put a foot on the threshold, Shane hit him savagely in the neck. Steele gave a strangled moan and slumped to the ground. Shane leaned against the wall, sobbing for breath for a moment or two and then he gripped Steele firmly by the collar and dragged him along the corridor and into the living-room.

The woman was standing in front of the fire, a glass in one hand. As he straightened up and turned, she threw herself on him, screaming with rage, her fingers clawing at his face. He lifted her in his arms, kicked open the bedroom door and dropped her on to the bed. On his way out he took the key and locked the door from the outside.

In the kitchen he found a length of clothes line, tied Steele's hands firmly behind his back and lifted him into one of the chairs by the fire. He helped himself to a drink and sat back and waited.

At first the woman hammered furiously on the bedroom door, but after a while she got tired. Steele groaned a couple of times and Shane leaned over and slapped him across the face. Steele's head snapped back and his eyes opened.

They wandered about the room aimlessly and then focused on Shane. For a moment longer they remained empty and vacant, and then a spark of anger appeared.

Shane filled a glass with whisky and threw it into Steele's face. 'That's better,' he said. 'Now we can talk.'

Steele's eyes burned with hate and his tongue

flickered over dry lips. 'I've got nothing to say to you,' he said.

Shane lit a cigarette. 'I think you have. I've been talking to Laura Faulkner. I saw you together the other night. She told me why.'

Something moved in Steele's eyes, but he shrugged and said calmly. 'I don't know what you're talking about.'

Shane's fist smashed into his mouth, jerked his head against the back of the chair. 'I haven't got much time,' he said. 'You've been blackmailing Laura Faulkner for years, you rat. You've got a certain envelope, addressed to her father, ready to be delivered if she doesn't do as she's told. I want it.'

Blood trickled from Steele's chin, staining his white shirt and his eyes were dark with hate. 'I'll pay you out for this, you bastard,' he screamed. 'You and that fancy bitch can go to hell.'

Shane reached for the poker and inserted it into the heart of the fire. 'As I said, I haven't got much time.' He sighed deeply and leaned back in his chair. 'It's funny how life goes round in a circle, isn't it? Here am I in exactly the same position as Colonel Li. He was in rather a hurry, too – remember?'

Steele was staring at the poker in fascinated horror and all colour had left his face. He tried to laugh. 'You wouldn't dare.'

Shane raised his eyebrows. 'But why not? I got the idea from your pal, Frenchy. He tried it on a friend of mine earlier this evening.'

There was a short silence and then Shane leaned forward and took the poker from the fire. It was white hot and he turned and smiled gently. 'Changed your mind yet, Reggie?'

Steele flung a curse at him and tried to scramble out of the chair. Shane flung him back and slowly advanced the poker. Sweat streamed down Steele's brow and his head moved frantically from side to side. For a moment Shane hesitated and then an expression of utter ruthlessness appeared on his face. Slowly and deliberately he extended his arm and Steele screamed, high and shrill like a woman 'Take it away. For Christ's sake, take it away.'

Shane lowered the poker, his face grim. 'The envelope,' he demanded. 'Where is it?'

'In the safe at my office,' Steele gabbled. 'Large white manilla envelope under the cash box on the top shelf. The key's in my right hand pocket.'

Shane's hand dipped into the pocket and came out holding a bunch of keys. He considered them for a moment and then slipped them into his own pocket. He grabbed Steele by the hair with his free hand and held the poker close to his cheek. 'Are you telling me the truth, you bastard?' he said menacingly.

Steele nodded frantically, a thin line of white

foam appearing on his lips. 'I swear I am,' he shrieked.

For a moment longer Shane held the poker threateningly and then he turned and threw it into the fireplace. Steele gave a great shudder of relief and fainted.

Shane walked across to the bedroom door and unlocked it. The woman was huddled on the bed. As he switched on the light, she sat up.

'I'm going now,' he said. 'You'd better see to your boy friend.'

'What have you done to him?' she demanded fearfully.

He shrugged. 'He'll be all right when you get him cleaned up.'

He returned to the living-room and she followed him slowly. There was a telephone on the table near the door and he ripped the flex from the connecting box on the wall and turned to the woman. 'I wouldn't try to get in touch with the police if I were you. I don't think Reggie would like that. I'm taking the car. Tell him I'll leave it outside the club.' She nodded mutely and he closed the door softly behind him and went along the dark corridor.

There was little traffic about and he drove alone with his thoughts and the steady hum of the engine. His back was paining him slightly and he leaned forward, trying to ease it a little. As he followed the main road into town, he suddenly realized that he was coming into the suburb in which the Faulkners lived. He slowed down a little, his eyes searching for the side road and then he saw it and swung the wheel sharply.

He left the car at the kerb and walked up the drive towards the house. It seemed to be in darkness and he followed the path around the side of the house and came out into the back garden.

As he approached the studio he could see a light and then the Dobermann started to bark and the sound was hollow and lonely and far away. Shane mounted the steps and stood there shaking his head from side to side as the sound of the dog seemed to fade away completely and then Laura Faulkner was framed in the doorway, looking at him inquiringly, her lips moving, but no sound issuing from them.

Complete panic moved inside him and he stretched out a hand to her. She pulled him inside and led him across to the divan. He slumped down, head in hands and after a while sounds returned to him and he straightened up slowly and looked at her anxious face.

'Just a dizzy spell,' he said. 'Nothing to get alarmed about.'

She dropped a hand on his shoulder. 'But you're wet through,' she said. 'What on earth have you been doing?'

He started to peel of his wet jacket. 'I've had a slight accident. You'd better get the first-aid kit out.'

He pulled off his shirt and she gave a sudden exclamation of horror when she saw his back. 'Martin, you're bleeding.'

'It's nothing serious,' he said. 'Just a few shot-gun pellets. Get a pair of tweezers and some surgical tape.'

She disappeared into the small kitchen and came back a moment later with a bowl full of hot water and a tin box. She sat down beside him on the divan. 'You need a doctor, Martin. It looks bad.'

He shook his head. 'It seems worse than it is. Clean my back and get to work with the tweezers. There shouldn't be many pellets there. I was lucky.'

As she gently cleaned away the blood with a flannel she said, 'What happened?'

He shrugged wearily. 'A difference of opinion with Reggie Steele. He was holed up in a cottage by the river at Hampton. When I got there he was pretty drunk. I told him I wanted those letters and he didn't seem to think it was such a good idea. We had words – that's where the shotgun came in – but I managed to make him see things my way in the end.'

She seemed to hesitate for a moment. 'Have you got the letters with you?'

He shook his head. 'I'll have them before long,

though.' He turned and smiled at her over his shoulder. 'Don't worry, angel. All your troubles are over.'

For a moment she gazed at him with something suspiciously like tears trembling in her eyes and then she took a deep breath and said; 'I'm going to use the tweezers now. I'll try not to hurt you.'

As he felt the first, sharp stabbing pain, he stifled a groan. 'How bad is it?'

'You were right,' she told him. 'It's nothing like as serious as it looked at first. There are three pellets a few inches apart, just under the skin.' He chewed hard on the corner of a cushion while she got the pellets out. As she started to clean the wounds she said, 'What happened to Reggie? Where is he now?'

'Still at the cottage,' he told her with a chuckle. 'Last I saw of him, he was looking decidedly the worse for wear in more ways than one.'

She quickly fixed strips of surgical tape in position and then got to her feet. 'You look all in,' she said. 'Lie back and put up your feet and I'll make you a cup of coffee, then I'll get you one of Dad's shirts.'

Suddenly Shane felt tired. He gently eased his sore back against a couple of cushions and lit a cigarette. He could hear her moving about in the kitchen and somehow the sound was comforting and right.

After a while she came in with a tray and placed it on a stool beside him. As she poured coffee into two cups she said, 'What do you intend to do next?'

He shrugged. 'I'll go down to the club and get those letters. Do you want to come with me?'

She shook her head. 'I'd like to, Martin, but it can't be done. I daren't leave my father on his own. He's not been at all well these last few days.'

As she poured cream into the coffee she went on, 'What will you do afterwards – about the other matter, I mean?'

Shane swallowed some of his coffee and sighed. 'I don't know, Laura. I don't know at all. Time is running out for me, and somehow the things that seemed important are meaningless now.'

'And what *is* important, Martin?' she said softly.

'You are,' he said.

She was sitting on the end of the divan gazing out of the window and now she turned her head slowly and looked directly at him. She was wearing a cardigan in a soft pink wool that clung to the curve of her breast and a superbly tailored skirt that fitted her like a second skin.

For a long breathless moment they looked at each other and then she put down her cup and got to her feet. She moved forward and stood beside him and then her hand reached out to the lamp and the room was plunged into darkness.

He lay there, his throat dry and listened to the rustle of her clothing as she undressed and then she was in his arms, her supple body melting into him and as he covered her face with kisses he could taste the salt of her tears upon his lips.

He was aware that he had slept, but for how long it was impossible to judge. The room was in darkness and he was alone and yet a faint, elusive trace of her perfume still hung upon the warm air.

His hand found the switch of the table lamp and the darkness retreated into the corners of the room. Shane swung his legs to the floor and yawned. There was a bad taste in his mouth and his back was still sore. He glanced at his watch. It was only a few minutes after midnight so he couldn't have slept for long.

He picked up his wet jacket and went to the door and opened it. When he went down the steps and walked up towards the house, the night air felt cold on his bare skin and he shivered and quickened his steps.

There was a light on in the kitchen and the Dobermann was curled up on a rug in a corner by the fire. He opened one eye and looked steadily at Shane for a moment and then closed it again, satisfied.

An airing rack festooned with various articles of laundry hung from the ceiling and Shane pulled down a white shirt and put it on quickly. It needed ironing badly, but it was clean and dry and he decided it would have to do him for the moment. He opened the other door and walked along the dark corridor which led towards the front of the house.

The hall was quiet and he walked towards the drawing-room door at the bottom of which a thin line of light showed and hesitated as he heard Laura speaking in a low voice. Very gently he turned the knob and opened the door.

She was standing facing him on the other side of a table, a telephone receiver in one hand. As he walked slowly forward she shook her head and said in a low voice, 'No, he was asleep when I left him.' And then she looked up and saw Shane.

Her face went pale and she quickly replaced the receiver in its cradle and forced a smile. 'Why, Martin, I thought you were still asleep.'

He walked round the table and stood very close to her. 'Who was that on the telephone just now?'

She shrugged. 'Just a friend. It was nothing important.'

She started to walk away and Shane grabbed her by the arm and pulled her close. 'You were discussing me with someone. Who was it?'

Suddenly she was angry and she struggled to free herself. 'You're hurting my arm,' she said.

He released her suddenly so that she fell back

against the table. She massaged her arm gently with one hand and glared at him. 'If you must know, I was speaking to Charles Graham about you.'

A sudden, cold rage erupted inside him. A rage that was compounded of disgust and loathing and bitter hurt. 'You're lying,' he said. 'You're lying.'

He slapped her heavily across the face and as she staggered back against the table, he moved forward and grabbed her by the shoulders. 'You're going to tell me the truth,' he said. 'I've had enough of lies and deceits.'

She started to struggle, her fingers clawing at his face and then the door swung open and her father appeared. He was wearing a dressing-gown and carried a walking stick in one hand. He lurched forward, raising the stick above his head and then, as he aimed a blow at Shane's head, he seemed to crumple at the knees and collapsed.

Shane lifted him in his arms and carried him across to the couch, all his rage evaporating. As he straightened up, Laura pushed him violently in the chest. 'Get out,' she screamed. 'Get out and don't come back. I never want to see you again.'

For a little while he stood staring into her face and then he turned without a word and walked out through the hall to the front door. She followed him and as he stepped on to the top step, the door slammed behind him and a bolt shot into place.

He stood there for a little while listening to her storm of weeping as she leaned against the other side of the door and then he walked down the drive towards the Daimler. His mind was completely frozen and he was only conscious of one thought. He was going to finish what he had started.

He drove fast on the way into town and as he turned the Daimler into the square and pulled up a few yards from the Garland Club, a church clock sounded one o'clock somewhere near at hand.

The fog was a little thicker and a steady drizzle was falling as he turned along the alley at the side of the club and moved towards the staff entrance. When he opened the door, the passage was deserted. He could hear the sound of voices from the kitchens and they were somehow muted and far away. He stood there for a moment listening and then he quickly mounted the back stairs to the first floor.

The corridor was deserted and he moved quickly along it to Steele's office. The door was locked and he took out the keys he had taken from Steele and tried them one by one. Behind him a door opened and there was a sudden burst of laughter. He moved across into the side passage quickly and flattened himself against the wall.

It sounded like some of the girls from the show and he listened to their voices fade along the corridor. When all was still again he moved back to the door and started again. The second key he tried fitted the lock and in a moment he was inside the room.

He switched on the light and went across to the safe which stood in the far corner next to the window. He inserted the most obvious key into the lock and the heavy door swung open to his touch. He pushed the cash box to one side and stood up, the manilla envelope clutched in his hands.

It was addressed in clear, rather feminine handwriting, to Henry Faulkner and Shane inserted a thumb under the flap to tear it open. At that moment he heard steps approaching along the corridor. He slipped the letter into his pocket and moved across the room quickly. He flattened himself against the wall a bare second before there was a knock on the door and it opened.

The man who had been on duty in the foyer on the first night Shane had visited the club, walked into the room. He was wearing a dinner jacket and carried a sheaf of papers in his hand. He frowned, his eyes travelling rapidly over the room and Shane took a quick step forward and smashed his fist into the unprotected jawline. As the man sank to the floor with a low groan Shane closed the door quietly and walked rapidly along the corridor.

When he emerged into the alley, the rain had

increased into a solid downpour. He moved towards the square and halted under the lamp that lighted the alley. His pulse was racing with excitement and he was filled with elation. He took out the manilla envelope, and tore open the flap.

He withdrew several sheets of paper. He unfolded the first one and held it up to the light of the lamp. It was filled with the same, rather feminine handwriting that he had first seen on the envelope and there was a heading at the top of the sheet – The True Facts Concerning The Death of Simon Faulkner.

Shane frowned and held the paper a little closer to his eyes. As he started to read, there was a faint movement behind him. Even as he turned, something thudded against the back of his neck, sending a wave of agony flooding into his brain to explode in a cascade of coloured lights.

The cobbles rose to meet him as he fell and he raised an arm to cover his face protectingly. There was no further blow. Someone stepped over him and the papers were plucked out of his hand and as Shane tried to struggle to his feet, his attacker disappeared into the fog, his club foot sliding over the wet pavement behind him.

Shane dragged himself up by the lamp-post and leaned against it, his head swimming. One thing above all others drummed its way insistently into his brain. The man with the club foot existed. He was real and not a fantasy conceived in the nightmare of his years of agony. He lurched towards the end of the alley as an engine coughed into life and a moment later, a car moved away through the fog. He slammed a hand against the wall in impotent fury and stayed there for a little while until he felt better.

He started to walk along the pavement, a peculiar deadness creeping through his limbs and the sounds of the traffic through the fog seemed to recede and grow still, leaving him alone in a vacuum of quiet. As he turned the corner into the main road, the pain moved inside his skull and he cried aloud in agony and grabbed for some iron railings.

It was worse – worse than he had ever known and he remembered what the specialist had told him. Severe pains, growing progressively worse heralded the final crisis and he moaned aloud in fear and staggered across the road to a taxi rank.

He gave the driver Jenny Green's address and crouched in the back seat, his head in his hands. When they reached the flat he thrust a pound note into the driver's hand and went up the drive towards the front door.

The stairs stretched into eternity and he went up them painfully on his hands and knees, clawing at the banister for support. When he reached the landing, he pulled himself upright and lurched across to the door.

It swung open to his touch and he managed to open his mouth and croak, 'Jenny?'

A hand grabbed him by the shoulders and he was hurled violently across the room. He tripped over a chair and fell heavily to the floor and as he closed his eyes against the white hot pain that moved behind them, he heard the slow dragging of the club foot as the limping man crossed the room. The door clicked softly as he went out and a moment later, Shane heard him descending the stairs.

He lay with his head pillowed against the carpet, hands tightly clenched together and it was with an effort that he finally opened his eyes.

There was blood on the carpet, a great wide, irregular stain and he stared at it in puzzlement and then struggled to his knees. His brain was going round in circles and he couldn't concentrate, but there was something wrong. There was something very wrong.

He turned his head slowly. There was blood everywhere, even on the walls as if some animal had been butchered. He tried to get up and fell forward on his face and his hand knocked against something hard. Lying on the floor in front of him was a razor sharp Ghurka kukri that he remembered had hung over the fireplace as an ornament. His fingers closed around the handle and he stared at the blood smeared blade dumbly and then a terrible light burst upon him and he cried out sharply, 'Jenny! Jenny, where are you?'

He found her in the other room sprawled across the bed. Her throat had been cut and her body was horribly mutilated. He stood at the side of the bed looking down at her and then a great wave of pain flooded through him and he fell across the bed beside her.

He was still lying there when the police found him, the kukri firmly clenched in his right hand.

14

It was raining when the police van turned in through the goods entrance of the station. The driver backed it against the end of the platform and Lomax jumped down from the cab and walked along the side of the vehicle. He clambered up on the platform and unlocked the rear door.

Shane stepped out flanked by two detectives. He was handcuffed to one of them by the right wrist and his coat was thrown loosely over his shoulders. The train was already in the station and they were standing opposite the guard's van. Shane smiled ironically and turned to Lomax. 'How long have we got?'

Lomax glanced at his watch. 'About ten minutes. How do you feel?'

Shane grinned. 'Like a cigarette.'

His face was pale and drawn in the lamplight. He drew gratefully on the cigarette that Lomax pushed into his mouth and sighed. 'That tastes good.' He laughed harshly. 'I suppose almost everything does at this stage in a man's life.'

Lomax frowned. 'I wouldn't think about it too much, if I were you. Perhaps this operation will be a success. Sir George Hammond is supposed to be the finest brain surgeon in Europe. A week from tonight you'll probably be lying in a bed in that hospital alive and kicking and wondering why you worried so much.'

'And afterwards you'll be able to send me for trial and have me hanged for a murder I didn't do,' Shane said. 'What a lovely prospect.'

Lomax shook his head. 'I don't think there's much danger of that.'

Shane turned on him, his face white and angry. 'Because I'm insane?' he demanded loudly. 'Is that what you mean? Is life imprisonment in Broadmoor a more attractive prospect?'

The young detective to whom he was handcuffed stirred uneasily and Lomax took Shane by the elbow and said calmly. 'Now don't start getting worked up again. I told you before that I thought you'd had a rotten break and I've tried to make things easy for you. I've done everything I can to help.'

'There's only one way you can help me,' Shane told him. 'Find the person who murdered Jenny Green.'

Lomax sighed. 'Now, don't let's start going over that again. It's all I've heard for the last two days. You're a sick man, Shane. You need help – medical help.'

Shane glared at him contemptuously. 'I suppose this is what you coppers like – an open and shut case and no need to wear out any shoe leather.'

He started to turn away and Lomax gripped him by the arm and jerked him round. The policeman's face was white and there was anger in his eyes. 'You listen to me,' he said, 'and listen hard. It may interest you to know that I've spent the last twelve hours checking on your story personally. I've visited every person you've had contact with since you arrived in this town.'

'And what did you find?' Shane demanded eagerly.

Lomax took out his pipe and filled it. 'That Reggie Steele was still at his cottage when the murder took place. His girl friend swears to that.'

Shane raised a clenched fist in a gesture of impotent fury. 'She'd swear her own mother's life away if she were offered enough. Couldn't you see that?'

'If it *was* Steele, how did he get to town so soon after you?' Lomax said. 'You took his car, remember?'

'Did you see Adam Crowther?' Shane asked.

Lomax nodded. 'He admitted that he lied to you. He did visit Reggie Steele at the Garland

Club, but only to warn him that you were in town and likely to cause trouble. To be perfectly frank, Crowther told me that he formed the opinion that you were unbalanced.'

'But it *could* have been Crowther,' Shane said. 'Everything fits. He's even lame in one foot – he lost his toes through frostbite in Korea.'

Lomax shook his head. 'He was working on something important at the university that night. Admittedly there was no one with him, but I'm satisfied he's telling the truth.'

'That's good,' Shane commented bitterly. 'That's bloody good. So you'll accept his word for it, will you? Why the hell shouldn't it be him? He's got a limp and the man who knocked me on the head in the flat had a limp. What makes Crowther so special?'

Lomax sighed heavily. 'All right, Shane,' he said. 'You've asked for it and you'll get it. I didn't finally accept Crowther's story until I'd spoken not only to Reggie Steele but to Charles Graham also. Steele doesn't have much time for you – he was honest enough to admit that – but Graham has. They both told me the same story – that you've been haunted by a memory for years. A memory named Colonel Li. He was the man with the club foot you heard that night in the flat, but he died in Korea seven years ago.'

Shane's breath hissed sharply between his teeth.

'There's nothing like being able to depend on one's friends for help. You must thank Graham for me next time you see him.'

There was anger in the policeman's eyes. 'It may interest you to know that Charles Graham is the man who's retained Sir George Hammond to perform your operation.'

There was a heavy silence. There didn't seem anything more to say, and then he remembered the girl. He said slowly, 'There's just one more thing I'd like to know, Inspector. Have you seen Laura Faulkner?'

Lomax nodded. 'We haven't bothered her too much. Her father had a stroke yesterday and they had to rush him into hospital. I understand it's only a matter of time.'

Before Shane could say anything the older of the two detectives moved forward and doors slammed hollowly along the train. Lomax nodded. 'Take him into the carriage now.'

They went towards the door, and as Shane put one foot on the step he hesitated, filled with a sudden wild urge to tell Lomax everything, to fill in all the gaps for him. One of the detectives pushed him firmly forward and the moment passed.

When they entered the reserved compartment, the young detective produced a key, freed himself from the handcuffs, and secured Shane's other wrist so that his hands were securely pinioned together in front of him. They pushed him into a corner seat, and one of them put his trench-coat up on the rack while the other knelt down and unlaced his shoes. Lomax stood in the doorway, keen eyes surveying everything. 'Did they give you a key for the door, Brown?' he asked the older of the two detectives. The man nodded, and Lomax went on, 'Keep the door locked at all times. They'll be waiting for you in London. I'll see you both tomorrow.'

As he started to turn away, Shane said quickly, 'Lomax!'

The inspector paused and looked over his shoulder. 'What is it?'

Shane smiled softly. 'You're wrong, you know.'

Lomax seemed about to speak, and then he shrugged and disappeared along the corridor. A moment later he passed the window and walked back towards the van.

Somewhere a whistle sounded, and the train seemed to give a long, shuddering sigh, and then they were gliding away from the platform, moving out into the rain and the darkness.

A feeling of complete panic surged through Shane. He stared down at his stockinged feet, at the handcuffs on his wrists, and a feeling of helplessness took possession of him. It was the end. Whichever way the dice fell he was finished.

He was brought back to reality sharply. Brown,

the detective with the key, had been trying to lock the compartment door, and now he straightened up and turned with a look of disgust on his face. 'The bloody thing won't fit,' he said.

The other man frowned and put down the newspaper he had opened. 'What are you going to do about it?'

Brown shrugged. 'I'll have to find the guard. He should have a master key.' He inclined his head towards Shane. 'Watch our friend here. You never know what his sort will try next.'

Shane turned and looked out of the window as Brown disappeared along the corridor. There was a slight ache behind his eyes and his guts churned over as the significance of Brown's words struck home. They thought he was insane. The whole thing was decided in advance. If he lived to stand in the dock, it would probably be the shortest trial on record.

In the darkness of the window he saw the reflection of the compartment behind him. The detective was watching him carefully, and after a while he moved along the seat and leaned over the lock.

Shane didn't even think about it. He swung round quickly and launched himself forward, his clenched fists raised high above his head. Even as the detective started to turn in alarm, they crashed into the back of his neck, and he fell forward from the seat and rolled on to the floor.

Shane wrench the sliding-door to one side and stepped over the prostrate figure. There was a sudden cry of alarm as Brown appeared at the far end of the carriage and started to run towards him.

Shane stumbled along the corridor and rounded the corner by the toilet. A door faced him with the communication cord stretched across the top of it. He yanked the cord firmly downwards with all his strength, and as the train started to brake to a halt, he struggled frantically with the handle of the door. It swung backwards suddenly as the wind caught it. He hesitated for a moment, straining his eyes into the blackness of the night, desperately trying to judge the train's speed. There was a cry behind him as Brown rounded the corner, and he hesitated no longer. As the detective's hand grabbed for his jacket, Shane jumped out into the night.

He tucked his head well into his shoulders and rolled over twice. As he tried to get to his feet, his own momentum was still carrying him forward and he fell on his face. The train was slowing to a halt a hundred yards away along the track, and as he struggled painfully to his feet he heard cries through the night and saw lanterns coming back along the track.

Beyond the train he could see the lights of the station in the darkness, and he realized, with something of a shock, that the whole business had happened in a matter of minutes.

He started to pick his way carefully across the lines, the stones digging into his stockinged feet painfully. He scrambled up a small embankment, and he pulled himself over a six-foot-high wooden fence at the top. He dropped down into a narrow street of terraced houses, and started to run.

The rain had increased into a solid downpour that bounced from the pavement. He seemed to be moving through an area of decaying slums, and he twisted and turned from one street into another until his lungs were heaving painfully and his throat was dry.

His head was aching slightly and his feet were torn and bleeding. Somewhere ahead of him he could hear the sounds of traffic, and guessed he was approaching the centre of the town. He paused on a corner and looked desperately about him, uncertain which way to go, and then a car rounded the corner and came towards him.

There was a narrow, dark opening in the opposite wall, and he crossed the street and plunged into it as the car flashed past. He started to move forward, his manacled hands held out in front of him. There was a lamp fastened high up on the brick wall, and beyond it he could see traffic passing along a busy street.

He leaned against the wall, his tortured lungs

clamouring for air, and as he looked up at the lamp it seemed to float away and become smaller and smaller, and then there was nothing but the darkness and he slid slowly down the wall into unconsciousness.

15

It was quiet in the vestry, and Shane stared out of the window into the darkness. Behind him Father Costello coughed and said softly, 'Is that all?'

Shane nodded slowly and turned towards him. 'That's it, Father,' he said. 'Right up to the moment I awakened behind the dustbin in that alley.'

The priest frowned, his slender fingers tapping thoughtfully on the desk top. 'It's a strange story,' he said. 'A very strange story.'

'But do you believe me, Father?' Shane said desperately. 'That's the important thing.'

Father Costello looked up at him searchingly, and suddenly he smiled. 'Yes, I think I do. Don't ask me why, but I don't think you killed her.'

Relief flooded through Shane and he sighed deeply. 'Thank God you do. I was beginning to wonder if they weren't right about me.'

Father Costello nodded and said soberly, 'That's

all very well, but it doesn't bring us any nearer to a solution. If you aren't the guilty one, then who did kill Jenny Green?'

Shane shook his head and sighed. 'I wish I knew, Father, I wish I knew.' He started to turn away, and then suddenly a great light burst upon him and he slammed a fist into his hand. 'There's just one way I might break this,' he said excitedly.

The priest leaned forward, interest leaping into his eyes. 'Tell me!' he said simply.

Shane lit a cigarette and his hand was trembling. 'If I'm sane and balanced and normal, then the man with the club foot exists. He wasn't simply a figment of my imagination. It was part of a deliberate attempt to make me think I was going out of my mind.'

'But how does all this help?' Father Costello demanded.

Shane frowned. 'I've just thought of a very simple way of finding out who he was.' He turned quickly and reached for a memo pad and pencil that were lying on the desk. 'There's more to it than that, but I haven't got time to explain now. You'll have to trust me, Father?'

He scribbled a name and address on the pad and pushed it across to the priest. 'I want you to give me exactly one hour, Father. No more, no less. Then I want you to ring Inspector Lomax at the C.I.D. and tell him I'm at this address.'

Father Costello looked at the address in surprise, and when he raised his head there was puzzlement in his eyes. 'Do you know what you're doing?'

Shane nodded. 'Will you do as I ask?'

The priest frowned down at the address, and then he sighed. 'On one condition.' He looked Shane directly in the eye. 'No killing. I must have your promise.'

Shane hesitated, a frown on his face, and then he shrugged. 'All right, Father. We'll play it your way.'

He opened the door and the priest said, 'Just a moment.' He took some keys from his pocket and threw them over. 'You'll find a car in the yard at the rear of the building. Not a very new model, I'm afraid, but you'll stand a better chance than you will on foot.'

Shane tried to speak, but for some reason the words refused to come, and the priest smiled faintly and made a slight gesture with one hand. 'Good luck!' he said, and Shane closed the door quickly and turned away.

He drove rapidly through the quiet streets into the centre of the town, and within minutes of leaving the church he was parking the car outside his hotel. The foyer was empty, and there was no one behind the counter. He moved forward quietly, and gently raised the flap of the reception desk. Someone was humming softly in the tiny office, and he slipped through the half-open door and closed it behind him.

The girl was standing in front of the mirror, applying a pencil to her eyebrows, and she turned in alarm. An expression of dismay appeared on her face, and her mouth opened to scream.

Shane jumped forward and clamped one hand over her mouth. 'Make a sound and it'll be your last, I promise you,' he said savagely. He released her, and she fell back against the desk, terror in her eyes.

She was wearing her new gaberdine suit, and Shane moved forward and fingered one of the lapels. 'I should have smelt a rat when I saw you wearing this the other day,' he said. 'You've never earned more than five quid a week in your life, and neither have any of your boy friends.'

She moistened her lips. 'It was a man I've only just met,' she said desperately. 'An older man. He's got plenty of money.'

Shane slapped her back-handed across the face. 'You're lying, you bitch,' he snarled. 'No man with that kind of money would ever give a little tramp like you a second glance. I'll tell you how you got that suit. Somebody paid you. Somebody who wanted to get into my room. They wanted a master key and you sold them one.'

Her face crumpled into pieces, and he knew that he was right. He caught hold of her hair and jerked back her head. 'Who was it?' he demanded.

She struggled to free herself, and there were tears in her eyes. 'I don't know the name,' she said. 'I was just handed the money in cash. I didn't mean any harm.'

Shane threw her back against the desk. 'Give me a description,' he said.

Slowly and hesitatingly, stumbling over her words, she began to speak. When she had finished, he sighed deeply and reached for a cigarette. The girl was crying, great sobs racking her body, and he looked at her coldly. 'Maybe this will teach you to keep your nose out of things that don't concern you in future.' He opened the door and said over his shoulder in a voice of deliberate venom, 'If you get on to the police about this, I swear I'll come back and cut your throat if it's the last thing I do on this earth.' She gave a little moan and sank down in the chair, and he closed the door and went outside to the car.

He drove boldly along the main street leading from the station, passing two policemen standing on a corner, and turned the car into St Michael's Square. The Garland Club was in darkness, and when he got out of the car and approached the entrance he found a notice on the door which stated that the club was closed temporarily.

He walked along the alley at the side of the

building and tried the staff door, but it was locked. He frowned, anxiety tugging at his heart, and moved into the yard at the rear of the building. As he looked up, a smile of relief appeared on his face as he saw the light showing through a chink in the curtains that covered the window of Steele's office.

Shane climbed on to a dustbin and jumped for the edge of the flat roof of the kitchens and pulled himself over the edge. He walked forward until he was standing outside the lighted window. There was a slight gap at the bottom and he listened, his ear close to it, for a second. There was no sound. He quietly inserted his fingers into the crack, took a deep breath and flung the window up. In almost the same instant he ripped the curtains aside and tumbled head first into the room.

Steele was sitting at the desk, and he turned in alarm, his hand dipping into a half-open drawer. Shane launched himself forward and rammed the drawer shut, trapping Steele's hand. Steele screamed and tried to rise, and Shane pulled open the drawer and slammed a fist into his face, knocking him to the floor.

His Luger was lying in the drawer, and he took it out and hefted it into his hand, his eyes on Steele. 'You never thought you'd see me again, you bastard – did you?'

Steele staggered to his feet, nursing his bruised

hand, and his face was curdled with fear. 'I'll give you anything,' he said frantically. 'Anything you like. I'll help you get away. Out of the country even. I've got friends. Only don't kill me! Don't kill me!'

He babbled on for several moments while Shane regarded him contemptuously, and finally he was silent, no more spirit left in him. Shane pushed him roughly towards the door. 'You and I are going for a little ride,' he said. 'I'd like you to meet a friend of mine. A good friend of mine. I think that between us we should manage to get the truth out of you.'

When they reached the car Shane told him to get behind the wheel and he sat in the passenger's seat beside him, a cigarette between his lips, and watched him carefully.

Steele didn't make the slightest attempt to resist as the car moved out through the suburbs and turned up the hill, leaving the lights of the city far behind in the rain. He followed Shane's orders implicitly, and when he turned off the engine of the car outside their destination he sat mutely behind the wheel waiting for further orders.

Shane opened the door and pulled him out, and together they mounted the steps to the front door. Steele looked ghastly. His mouth was smashed and bleeding, and the front of his shirt was soaked in blood. There was a kind of hopelessness in his eyes, and he leaned against the wall, his breathing shallow and irregular and waited as Shane rang the bell.

The door opened, throwing a shaft of yellow light into the night, and Charles Graham peered out into the night. Shane pushed Steele forward and followed him in. An expression of alarm appeared in Graham's eyes, and he quickly closed the door. 'Shane!' he cried in amazement. 'But what's happened? I thought you were supposed to be on your way to London?'

Shane nodded grimly. 'That's what a lot of people thought, but I'd other ideas myself.' He pushed Steele forward. 'I want the answers to some questions, and this pig is going to give them to me.' He turned to Graham and smiled tightly. 'I don't like involving you like this, Graham, but I need your help badly. Could we go upstairs?'

Graham nodded. 'Of course, Shane. But I hope you know what you're doing.'

He led the way upstairs to the conservatory, and Shane followed, pushing Steele in front of him. The scent of the orchids and the intense heat were almost overpowering, and as they entered the great glass room beads of sweat appeared on Shane's brow and trickled down into his eyes.

Graham was wearing a thin nylon shirt and silk scarf. He looked relaxed and comfortable as he led the way along the path to the terrace end of the conservatory. He sat on the edge of the table and faced them. His scarred face showed no expression, but his eyes were worried. 'Now then,' he demanded. 'I suppose you're accusing Steele of having murdered that girl, but how exactly do you intend to prove it?'

Shane smiled faintly and reached for a cigarette. He lit it quickly and blew out a long column of smoke. He felt completely relaxed and assured, and his hand dipped into his pocket and came out holding the Luger.

'But I don't think it was Steele who murdered the girl,' he said softly. 'I think it was you, Graham.'

Somewhere in the distance thunder rumbled ominously, and the rain increased in a sudden rush that hammered against the glass roof of the conservatory. There was no change of expression on Charles Graham's face. He lit a cigarette and said calmly, 'Are you quite sure you know what you're saying?'

Steele took a quick step forward and his voice was high-pitched and cracking with fear. 'I warned you,' he cried. 'I said he was dangerous.'

Graham's iron control snapped, and he slapped him savagely across the face. 'Get a grip on yourself, you damned fool!'

Steele went completely to pieces. He whirled round and flung himself on Shane, eyes rolling horribly, saliva trickling from the corner of his mouth. Shane took a quick pace backwards and kicked him in the stomach.

As Steele writhed on the floor, Graham moved forward and looked down at him contemptuously. 'I should have got rid of him a long time ago.'

Shane covered him with the Luger. 'Sit down,' he said deliberately. The bell which sounded from the front door was fixed to a wooden post near by, and he wrenched the connecting wires from the terminal box and grinned tightly. 'Now we can talk without being interrupted.'

Graham sat on one of the basket-chairs, hands clasped in front of him. He looked completely calm and self-assured. 'I'd be interested to know how you got on to me.'

Shane leaned back against one of the iron pillars which supported the roof. 'In the beginning I suspected everybody. Crowther, Steele – even Laura Faulkner – but the pieces didn't seem to fit. The truth only came to me an hour ago. I went back over everything, searching desperately for a clue – anything that would help me to make sense out of things. It was then that I remembered two significant points, both of which tied you in with Steele.'

Graham reached for another cigarette. 'And what were they?'

'It was really Steele who gave the game away,'

Shane said. 'On that first night when I went to see him at the Garland Club he referred to the fact that I'd been in an institution. When I threatened him he told me I'd better watch my step or I might easily find myself back in the madhouse. I'd only told two people about that – you and Laura Faulkner.'

'Very interesting,' Graham said, 'but hardly conclusive.'

'Not on its own, but I remembered another curious fact. The night I broke into Steele's office to look for the envelope which supposedly contained Laura Faulkner's letters, he was waiting for me in the dark with a couple of his strong-arm boys. There was only one possible explanation for that. He was expecting me because someone had warned him I might be coming. You were the only person who knew.'

Graham shook his head and something like a smile touched his twisted mouth. 'Highly interesting,' he said, 'But also highly circumstantial. None of it would stand up in court. After all, Laura Faulkner knew you were hoping to get hold of that envelope.' He shook his head. 'You'll have to do better than that.'

'But I can,' Shane said softly. 'I've still got my ace-in-the-hole. I had a private word with the receptionist at my hotel earlier this evening. She suddenly started spending money on clothes –

a lot of money. I wondered if there was any connexion between that and the fact that someone had been able to obtain a key which let them into my room. Whoever it was, stole my Luger. I found it in Steele's office.'

'Then why blame me?' Graham said.

'Because after I slapped her around a bit, the girl described you perfectly,' Shane told him. 'And let's face it. That wouldn't be a difficult thing to do.'

'So I killed Jenny Green?' Graham said.

'You were the only person I'd told that I was staying at her flat.' Shane said. 'Steele's strong-arm boys knew because you must have told Steele, but they were out of action. In the state in which I left Steele, he couldn't possibly have reached town in time. I even considered Adam Crowther, but he knew nothing about my relationship with Jenny Green. It had to be you, Graham. Simple arithmetic. You were the only one left.' Shane frowned as a tiny pain started to move behind his right eye. 'The only thing I can't understand is why?'

Graham sighed and started to rise from his chair and Steele rolled over feebly and clutched at Shane's legs. Shane stumbled on to one knee and Graham jumped forward and neatly wrenched the Luger from his hand. Shane vainly grabbed at his arm. His fingers clawed at the sleeve and as Graham stepped back, the thin nylon material shredded and the entire sleeve came away in Shane's hand.

In the silence that followed, Shane's breath hissed sharply between his teeth and the moist air of the conservatory seemed to move in on him with a terrible weightless pressure.

Graham held the Luger at waist height, his bare right arm white against the blue of his shirt. There was only one thing wrong. Around his forearm was tattooed a red and green snake and underneath it the legend: Simon and Martin – friends for life.

Out of the silence Steele cried feebly, 'Let him have it, Faulkner. It's either him or us.'

Shane got to his feet and leaned back against the iron pillar. The pain in his head was much worse and when he ran a hand over his face it was damp with sweat. When he finally spoke his voice sounded as if it came from a great distance. 'What happened, Simon?' he said. 'What really happened?'

'In Korea you mean?' Simon Faulkner shrugged. 'I was the one Colonel Li picked out of the hat for his shooting gallery. I wanted to live – it was that simple. He had the firing party sound off outside to fool the rest of you and returned me to my cell. Later on he told me they had a further use for me. To act as a spy in the prison camps in the North.'

'And didn't that worry you?' Shane said.

Faulkner shrugged. 'I didn't have much time to think about it because the Americans started bombing the place almost immediately after that.'

'And how did you manage to get away?' Shane said.

Faulkner shrugged. 'Exactly as I told you when you first came to see me.' He laughed suddenly. 'Everything seemed to be working out perfectly for me and then I stepped on that land mine.'

'But how did you manage the identity switch with Charles Graham?'

Faulkner grinned and put another cigarette between his twisted lips. 'I didn't have to do a thing about it,' he said. 'It just happened. When I came round in hospital, I couldn't speak, I couldn't even see. It was then that somebody called me Charles Graham. At first I was too weak to contradict. I knew Graham was dead because I'd seen what was left of him after the bombing. After a while I realized what had happened. The uniform I'd snatched up in Colonel Li's office was Graham's and that's how they'd identified me.'

He laughed harshly. 'A little later they brought in the colonel of the regiment. When he didn't recognize me and started rambling on about the wonders they could do with plastic surgery these days, I suddenly realized how simple everything was. There was the money and the business Graham had been left by his uncle and he had no other relatives. The plastic surgery would account for the change and the rest of you were all dead on the hill in the ruins of that blasted temple.'

Shane was beginning to feel tired – very tired and the pain in his head was worse. It was an effort to speak and he shook his head slightly and said, 'You were still taking a hell of a chance.'

Simon Faulkner nodded. 'But then it was worth it. You see, I had at least five years facing me when I got back home. I'd rather unwisely gambled on the stock exchange with large sums of money from the firm. I knew it was bound to come out in a matter of weeks. That's why I volunteered for Korea.'

'I know,' Shane told him. 'Your sister told me all about that.' A thought suddenly occurred to him and he said with a slight frown, 'Tell me something – did Laura know about this?'

Faulkner nodded. 'Yes, I made rather a bad slip. When they'd got through with me at that Plastic Surgery Unit, I was confident that even my own mother couldn't have connected me with the man who walked out of there. I decided to put it to the test. I wrote to Laura, explaining that I'd been in Korea with her brother and she invited me to visit the house.'

'And she recognized you?' Shane demanded incredulously.

'Believe it or not it was my handwriting she

recognized,' Faulkner laughed. 'Fate added a nice touch of irony there.'

'And you admitted everything to her?'

Faulkner nodded. 'There didn't seem to be any point in denying it and I was perfectly safe. She didn't want another scandal. It would have killed my father.'

'When did things really begin to go wrong?' Shane said.

Faulkner shrugged. 'When the end of the war came and the Chinese started to release prisoners. I took the bull by the horns and went to see Crowther when he came home. He didn't suspect anything for an instant. Reggie Steele came to see me before I could visit him. He let me put on quite a performance for five or ten minutes and then announced that he knew damn well who I really was. He'd been lying in the rubble, pinned by his legs. He'd seen me leave the temple in one piece.'

'And you had to pay for his silence?'

Faulkner nodded. 'At first I looked for a way to get rid of him, but then he opened his club and I began to see the possibilities in our association. I provided the brains and he was the figure-head. We've made a lot of cash during the last few years.'

'Did you know he was blackmailing your sister?' Shane said.

Faulkner shook his head. 'I'm afraid Laura acted very foolishly there. Steele threatened to expose me to my father if she didn't play ball with him. She's suffered needlessly for years. All she had to do was tell me and I could have stopped it by lifting the phone, but then – she didn't know of my association with Steele.'

Shane was finding it difficult to concentrate. He frowned and passed a hand over his brow. 'What about Wilby? Where did he fit in?'

Faulkner sighed. 'That was Steele's mistake, I'm afraid. It made him feel big to give Wilby a job for old time's sake when he came whining, cap in hand.'

'Presumably he discovered your secret?'

Faulkner nodded. 'He overheard us talking in Steele's office one evening. It was easy enough to keep his mouth shut. In the first place, he was frightened to death of me and in the second, he was perfectly happy as long as he had enough money to get drunk on. Unfortunately the picture changed for the worse when you appeared on the scene.'

'You put him in that gas oven?' Shane said.

Faulkner nodded tranquilly. 'All of a sudden he was more afraid of you than he was of me. He wrote me a letter in which he said he couldn't stand it any more. He was going to tell you every-thing. I went to his house prepared to offer him a bribe large enough to keep his mouth shut until I'd managed to get rid of you one way or another.'

'And what went wrong?' Shane said.

Faulkner shrugged. 'I found him drunk in the kitchen. It was too good an opportunity to miss. I dragged him across to the gas oven and put his head inside.'

'But how did you manage the suicide note?' Shane asked.

Faulkner smiled. 'The final touch of artistry, I left the second page of the letter he had written to me. It looked like a brief note and in it, he referred to you quite damningly.'

'And all the other things,' Shane said. 'The footsteps and the incident in the fog when I saw Laura going into that hotel? You were behind them all?'

'The club foot seemed a nice touch,' Faulkner said. 'After all you appeared to have Colonel Li on the brain and there was no need to kill you. You were going to die anyway. I thought that if I could make you think your reason was going you might leave.'

'But how about that business at the hotel when Laura vanished?'

'I didn't want her visiting my house in case you happened to drop by unexpectedly,' Faulkner said. 'I arranged to meet her at that hotel. I was watching from the window and saw you following her. I phoned down to the desk and told the hall porter exactly what to do. I said we were having an affair and you were a nosy private detective employed by the husband.'

'That still doesn't explain the phone call I made to her house.'

Faulkner chuckled. 'But you didn't make the phone call – the hall porter dialled the number for you. In actual fact he connected you to the room upstairs where we were meeting.'

Everything had dropped neatly into place, but the picture was still incomplete. Shane said slowly, 'And what about Jenny? Why did you have to kill her?'

Faulkner shrugged. 'But surely that's obvious? I wanted rid of you once and for all. After you left Steele at Hampton he managed to call me from a public phone box on the main road. He told me you were going to the club to get that envelope from the safe and he told me what was in it. Not letters from Laura to him as she had told you, but the truth about me. A few minutes later Laura phoned to tell me the same thing. She said that she'd managed to delay you at the house. She wanted me to get to that envelope before you could open it.'

There was no hurt in the knowledge, only a certain sadness and something suspiciously like regret. Shane swallowed hard and said slowly, 'I see.'

Faulkner shook his head. 'No, you don't see at all, Martin. I knew Laura had fallen for you pretty heavily, but stronger than that was her desperate resolve to see that the truth about me was never revealed. She knew it would kill my father.'

'But none of this explains why you killed Jenny,' Shane said.

'After I'd clubbed you down in the alley, I realized that you'd make for the girl's flat and then I suddenly thought of a way in which I could get rid of you once and for all. You'd been in an institution for years and several people knew of your obsession that one of your comrades had been a traitor in Korea. You'd even been publicly rebuked by the coroner at Wilby's inquest. All I had to do was to get to the flat before you, murder the girl and club you down when you came in.'

'But you didn't just murder her, you bastard,' Shane said. 'You butchered her.'

'But I had to do it that way,' Faulkner said patiently. 'You were suspected of being insane. It had to be that sort of murder.'

Steele had managed to struggle to his feet and he slumped into one of the chairs, his face bone white and drawn with pain. 'What are we going to do with him?' he said.

Faulkner shrugged. 'I'm going to shoot him,' he said calmly. 'It's very simple. He forced you to bring him here from the club. He had a gun. There was a struggle and I managed to shoot him.'

Shane took a deep breath and tried to straighten his tired body and then there was a sudden movement in the shrubbery behind him and Lomax moved forward and stood at his shoulder.

Shane felt a tremendous relief flooding through him and he sagged back against the pillar. 'What kept you?' he said. 'I was beginning to get worried.'

Lomax grinned. 'I've been here for quite a while,' he said. 'There was no reply when I rang the bell at the front door so I had to force a window. You were so busy talking you didn't hear me come in.'

'Did you get it all?' Shane said.

Lomax nodded. 'Enough – I'll apologize to you later.' He turned to Faulkner and said grimly. 'You'd better hand that thing over – the house is surrounded anyway. You wouldn't get very far.'

Steele gave a cry of dismay and tried to get to his feet. Faulkner turned quickly and slashed him across the head with the barrel of the Luger and then he moved back until he was leaning against the door which led out on to the terrace.

'The first man to move gets a bullet between the eyes,' he said, 'and I mean it. I've nothing to lose and I don't intend to hang.'

He opened the door to the terrace and as he stepped backwards, his eyes never leaving them, Shane said gently, 'But you *are* going to hang, Simon. You see I promised a friend of mine earlier in the evening that I wouldn't kill you. As I didn't trust myself not to pull the trigger when I had the gun trained on you, I thought I'd better take safety precautions.' His hand came out of his pocket and he held up the magazine from the Luger.

Faulkner's whole body seemed to go rigid and then his tortured face twisted with fury. 'You're lying!' he said furiously and pulled the trigger. The empty, metallic click echoed through the silence and Shane began to walk slowly towards him.

Behind him Lomax cried out in dismay and clutched at his shoulder but Shane shook him off. He was not conscious of anything except Faulkner's eyes burning with hate from his ravaged face. This was something personal, something that had to be settled between the two of them.

Faulkner backed slowly away along the terrace, the Luger held out uselessly in front of him. He glanced over his shoulder once and when he turned to face Shane again there was a gleam of hope in his eyes. Shane looked beyond him and saw the iron ladder of the fire-escape and shook his head slowly. 'You won't escape me, Simon,' he said. 'This is the final ending to the story. This is the moment when all debts are paid.'

Faulkner suddenly flung the Luger at him with all his strength. Shane tried to duck, but it caught him a glancing blow high on the forehead and he cried aloud in agony as something seemed to move inside his brain and the night exploded into coloured lights.

He staggered forward, his hands groping blindly in front of him and Faulkner jumped up on to the balustrade and reached for the ladder. Shane's right hand secured a grip on an ankle and he pulled. He glanced up and was conscious of the monstrous face glaring down at him, and then Faulkner kicked at him savagely with his other foot.

Shane staggered back, cannoning into Lomax, and Faulkner's foot slipped and he stepped backwards into space. For a moment he seemed to poise there and then he screamed horribly and disappeared.

The sound of that scream seemed to penetrate into Shane's brain where it whirled round and round in a decreasing circle and then the light that streamed from the windows seemed to grow into a large ball that started to spin round and round in front of his eyes until it exploded and he plunged into darkness.

16

It was quiet when he awoke – very quiet and he found himself in unfamiliar surroundings. He was lying in a narrow hospital bed and the walls of the small room and its furniture were all painted white.

After a while he tried to sit up. For some unaccountable reason his head felt detached from the rest of his body and when he raised a hand to his forehead, he encountered a heavy bandage.

He tried to push himself up even further and at that moment the door opened and a nurse entered the room. She was a large, middle-aged woman with a pleasant face and large, capable hands. She moved forward quickly and gently pushed him back against the pillows. 'You mustn't do that,' she said. 'You mustn't even move.'

'Where am I?' Shane said weakly. 'What happened?'

Jack Higgins

'You're in a private room at Burnham General Infirmary,' she said. 'You've been here for the past five days.'

Shane frowned. 'Five days?' he said. 'But I don't understand.'

She smoothed the sheets quickly and lifted a temperature chart from a hook on the wall. 'You've had a very serious operation. It's a miracle you're here at all.'

For a moment her voice seemed to recede into the distance, leaving him alone as he considered the implication of her words and then he took a deep breath and said slowly, 'Are you trying to tell me that I've had the operation that was needed to remove shrapnel from my brain?'

She nodded. 'That's right. You were brought in here in a terrible state. Sir George Hammond flew up specially from London to perform the operation. He was hoping you'd regain consciousness before he left, but he had another important operation in Germany so he had to leave yesterday.'

'So I'm not going to die after all?' Shane said slowly.

She laughed cheerfully. 'Good heavens no. You'll be here for a week or two yet, but you'll be perfectly fit when you leave.'

She went out of the room and he lay back against the pillows and stared up at the ceiling, suddenly feeling drained of all emotion. Perhaps

208

at some later time he would feel elation, but at the moment he was conscious of nothing – only of an emptiness, a coldness that moved inside him and was not to be explained.

A few minutes later a doctor came in to see him and gave him a routine examination and afterwards, the nurse brought him something to eat.

As she was arranging the tray across his knees, he noticed some flowers in a vase by the window and asked her who had brought them. She smiled. 'They were from the young lady,' she said. 'Miss Faulkner, I think the name is.'

Shane tried to sound casual and unconcerned. 'She's been here?'

'Every day,' the nurse told him. 'I've promised to phone her the moment you come round.'

After she'd taken the tray away, he lay back against the pillow, staring out through the window at the driving rain and thinking about Laura Faulkner. His senses seemed sharper, more acute than he had ever known them before. He could even smell the perfume of the flowers from across the room and he was filled with an aching longing for her. The door clicked quietly open and he turned eagerly.

Lomax was standing there, a light smile on his face. 'You look disappointed,' he said. 'Expecting someone else?'

Shane grinned weakly. 'I thought it might be Laura Faulkner.'

Lomax shook his head. 'Her father was brought in here the same day you were,' he said. 'He died yesterday. I understand the funeral is this morning. She'll probably be pretty busy.'

Shane's hand tightened over the edge of the sheets and he cursed softly thinking of her on her own. He pushed the thought away from him and said, 'Got a cigarette?'

Lomax handed him a cigarette and said, 'She's got a lot of guts that girl. They buried her brother three days ago and she followed the coffin right to the graveside. That took some doing under the circumstances. From what I can make out he never did much for her or the old man.'

Lomax gave him a light. Shane inhaled gratefully and sighed. 'I never thought I'd live to enjoy things like this again.' He gestured to a nearby chair. 'Sit down and fill me in on what's happened.'

Lomax took out his pipe. 'There's nothing much to tell. Faulkner was killed instantly by his fall. Steele's in custody. We've got him for being an accessory before the fact of at least one murder and a string of other criminal charges. We found some very interesting things when we searched his office. He and Faulkner had their fingers in just about everything from organized prostitution to dope peddling.'

Shane frowned and half-closed his eyes. He tried hard to visualize Simon Faulkner. Simon the good comrade, steady and dependable in a tight corner, always gay and smiling. But it was no use. The memory had become somehow elusive and unreal as if it had been nothing more than a figment of his imagination.

He shook his head helplessly. 'It shows how little we know anyone – even our closest friends.' He half-smiled. 'And what about me? No assault charges? What about that young constable in the alley and the detective on the train? I'm afraid I didn't have time to be gentle.'

'Technically I could book you, but under the circumstances . . .' Lomax shrugged and got to his feet.

'I'll see you again before I leave, I hope,' Shane said.

Lomax nodded. 'You can buy me a pint the day you come out.' He grinned. 'I must be off. You can lie here in bed if you like, but as far as I'm concerned one crime starts where another finishes.'

As he opened the door, Shane said, 'Lomax – about Faulkner.' The detective turned and regarded him curiously and Shane continued. 'He wasn't all bad, you know. He saved my life once. I got shrapnel in my foot and he carried me in on his back under heavy fire.'

Lomax shrugged. 'Like you said, who knows

what goes on in the mind of any human being?' He waved a hand in a small gesture of futility that summed the whole thing up and the door closed softly behind him.

Shane lay staring at the ceiling, thinking about Simon Faulkner and after a while the door opened quietly and Father Costello appeared. He was wearing a dark raincoat and carried a black bag in his right hand. He smiled warmly and sat on the edge of the bed. 'It does my heart good to see you back in the land of the living, Martin.'

'Thanks to you, Father,' Shane told him. 'If you hadn't had faith in me . . .' His voice trailed away into silence.

'Nonsense,' Father Costello said. 'The truth always comes out in the end if we have a little faith.' He got to his feet. 'I'm sorry I can't stay. Laura Faulkner's father died yesterday. The funeral is this morning and she's asked me to officiate.'

Shane swallowed hard. 'How is she, Father?'

The priest shrugged. 'This thing has hit her harder than anything else, Martin. First her brother and the scandal of what he was and did, and now her father.' He sighed heavily and walked to the door. 'I'll tell her I saw you, Martin. If she comes to see you be gentle with her. Poor girl, she's quite alone.'

After he had gone Shane lay staring out of the window, thinking about Laura Faulkner and after a while he threw back the bedclothes and swung his feet to the floor. When he stood up and walked across to the wardrobe, he felt as if he were floating and there was a slight buzzing in his ears.

His clothes were hanging neatly from several hangers and he changed as quickly as he could. It took him quite a while to fasten the various buttons and, as his hands were trembling so much, he decided not to bother with a tie. He pulled on his trench-coat and walked across to the door.

The corridor was deserted and he moved quickly along it and went down the stairs at the far end. On the ground floor there seemed to be a great many people moving about, some in uniform, but many of them patients. He moved steadily along a corridor that emptied into a pleasant, tiled foyer and facing him was a wide glass door.

A porter in blue uniform and peaked cap was standing in the porch looking out at the rain and Shane said, 'Excuse me, I understand someone was being buried from the hospital this morning – a Mr Faulkner. Has the cortege left yet?'

The porter turned and looked at him curiously. 'About fifteen minutes ago, sir.'

'Have you any idea where the burial is to take place?' Shane said.

'St Augustine's, I believe,' the porter replied. He frowned suddenly as Shane half-closed his eyes and swayed a little. 'Are you all right, sir?'

Shane nodded. 'Nothing to worry about. I'm not long out of bed, that's all.' He moved down the steps quickly before the porter could inquire further and waved for a cab from the nearby rank.

When they reached the church, he told the driver to wait for him and walked slowly through the gate and along a narrow path lined with poplar trees which led to the cemetery.

He could hear Father Costello's voice as he went forward and then he saw them. There were no more than half a dozen people grouped round the grave and the priest's voice sounded brave and strong as the rain fell on his bare head.

Shane moved off the path and stood behind a large, marble monument. Laura was standing on the far side of the grave. She wore a black, close fitting suit and there were dark smudges under her eyes. The Dobermann sat beside her and Shane saw that she had one hand fastened firmly about the dog's collar as if he were the last friend she had left on top of earth.

Shane recoiled at the horrid sound the first spadeful of wet earth made as it rattled against the coffin. He shivered and turned away and walked quickly between the gravestones that reared out of the clammy earth, back towards the gate.

He sat in the cab and waited and after a while they came through the gate. Father Costello talked to her for a moment or two, holding her hand, his face kind and gentle and then she got into a hired car with the dog and they drove away.

Shane told his driver to follow and leaned back against the cushions and lit a cigarette. His body was trembling slightly and the smoke made him feel sick. He tossed the cigarette out of the window and wiped cold sweat from his brow with the back of his hand. He had no idea of what he was going to say to her. He was only sure of one thing. He needed her more than he had ever needed anything or anybody in his life before.

The hired car dropped her at the gate of the house and Shane waited until she had disappeared through the gate before paying off his driver and following her.

The place seemed more derelict than ever and the curtains were drawn across the windows, giving them somehow the appearance of great, sightless eyes that looked blindly down at him.

He walked round the side of the house and down towards the studio. The rain increased with a sudden rush into a torrential downpour and a rook lifted out of the trees above the river, protesting shrilly. Shane mounted the steps to the studio and opened the door.

The Dobermann moved across the room like a dark shadow, a growl dying in its throat and unexpectedly nuzzled his hand. Laura Faulkner had been standing by the great glass window and she turned quickly.

Her eyes looked somehow too large in her fine-drawn face. She gazed incredulously at him and then a tiny moan escaped from her mouth and she took a hesitant step forward.

In a moment she was in his arms and he held her close as a storm of weeping engulfed her. After a while she stopped crying and looked up at him with a wan smile. 'Should you be out of hospital?'

He grinned. 'They're probably going crazy at the moment, but that doesn't matter. I wanted to see you.' There was a slight pause and he said, 'I'm sorry about your father.'

She sighed and moved away from him. 'I'm not, now that it's all over. It hasn't been much of a life for him during these last few years.'

'Or for you,' Shane said.

She took a deep breath. 'Before we go any further there are one or two things you should know. I knew that Charles Graham was really Simon.'

'I know,' Shane said gently. 'Simon told me just before he died.'

'But there's one other thing you should know,' she said in an expressionless voice. 'The night you came here after making Steele give you the key to his safe and told me you intended going to his office for the letters. I warned Simon. That's what I was doing when you surprised me on the telephone.'

'I know that, too,' Shane told her.

For a moment she registered surprise and then her shoulders slumped and she said wearily. 'I don't expect you to believe me, but I didn't know about the other things. I didn't realize he was trying to drive you insane.'

Shane took a quick step forward and pulled her close. 'But I *do* believe you,' he said.

She gazed up at him in wonder and then shook her head. 'But why should you?'

He shrugged. 'Because I love you. I think I loved you on that first day. And I need you desperately, just as much as you need me. We've both been reborn in a way and birth is a painful process. The most painful of all. It's not going to be easy for either of us to pick up the threads of a new life on our own.'

For a timeless moment she gazed up at him and there were tears in her eyes and then she smiled and taking his hand, tugged him towards the door.

'Where are we going?' he demanded in bewilderment.

'To get my car,' she said firmly. 'You're going straight back to hospital.'

For a moment he was going to argue, but she looked up at him belligerently. He laughed softly, feeling suddenly happy for the first time in years, and together they walked up the path towards the house with the Dobermann trailing at their heels.